BUCKING THE SYSTEM

by Dragon Cobolt
Characters, Illustrations, and Editing by Kadath

Bucking the System

Copyright © 2019 by Dragon Cobolt
Production © 2019 FurPlanet Productions
Cover Artwork and illustrations © Kadath 2019
http://www.furaffinity.net/user/Kadath

Published by FurPlanet Productions
Dallas, Texas
www.FurPlanet.com

Print ISBN 978-1-61450-517-4
eBook ISBN 978-1-61450-518-1

First Edition Trade Paperback 2019

TABLE OF CONTENTS

CHAPTER 1

"My day was bracketed by the two of them. The events went into motion when I saw her off and later met him."

* * *

The rain that had swept through the previous night left a pleasant scent to the air, which drifted in through the open window of Patrick's London flat. The lean, muscular giraffe woke up before his jackal lover, Nadia. She lay sprawled out beside him, her luxurious dark gray-furred body barely covered by a thin, silk sheet. The fabric was so smooth and sheer that it was able to cling to every rise, every dipping canyon, every curve of her luscious body. Pat spent a few moments simply marveling that he was in the same bed as this goddess, his cock getting harder and harder by the moment as the beauty breathed quietly, head turned against her pillow, tail twitching gently in her dreams.

Nadia was not the only name she went by, and was one she rarely preferred. A former dominatrix, she had gone under the moniker Nightshade, which she retained for her current job as an exotic dancer at the Safari club—one of the most popular gentlemen's clubs in London. They had met there over a year ago, and Pat was just as in awe of her grace and allure now as he had been when he first set eyes on her.

Nadia opened one eye and grinned at him. It was a fierce, predatory grin.

"Can we do it in the shower?" Pat asked, before Nadia suddenly sprang on him. She considered, then nodded casually, as if she were granting some great favor to a lowly peasant. Since this was her, it might as well have been.

* * *

The pattering sound of the water slipping off Pat's balls was only the third loudest sound in the shower. His hands clenched Nadia's luscious hips as he ducked his head over her shoulder, grunting quietly as his cock slammed into her sex, the wet *slap slap slap* of their meeting hips sending echoes throughout the room. That was the second sound. The loudest, however, was Nadia herself. Her nails dug between the linoleum tiles of the shower, her head tilting back as she moaned. "Fuck me! Fuck me *harder...* ah!" Her tone was utterly dominant, and Pat could feel the tightness of her sex as he thrust deep and fast. He panted, eyes closed, and tried to follow his mistress's orders.

Former dominatrix. Exotic dancer. Utter size queen. These were things that could describe Nightshade. Being uncommunicative wasn't one of them.

Pat reached forward and found her clit, rubbing it insistently with his fingers. Nadia shuddered, hanging her head forward. "*Fuck,*" she growled, her sex clenching. Pat tried to hold back, but couldn't. His balls clenched and his cock jerked as he felt his seed rushing to fill Nadia's pussy. Some dripped out from around Pat's cock, joining the water pattering down the drain. Nadia panted and laughed shakily.

"You fuck all right," she said, her voice casual, airy, for all the world sounding like she hadn't just been fucked. "For a *dork.*"

Pat laughed. "You're never going to forgive me for quoting movies in bed, are you?" He stuck his tongue out at her. Nadia grinned, then reached up and turned the shower knob in a quick circle before moving out of the way. Pat squeaked as the water went from warm to freezing.

* * *

Once he was out of the shower, dried, and dressed, he kissed Nadia on the cheek. "So," he said, "I may be home late today. No idea how long the interview is going to be."

"Who are you interviewing again?" she asked, sliding on the thick black coat she wore to get to the Safari, tucking her phone into her biggest pocket.

Pat grinned, puffing up his chest. "Ezra Maes!" he said, spreading out one hand in the air, as if he was gesturing to a marquee with the name in twelve foot high, illuminated letters. He looked at Nadia, ready for her to be shocked, excited and thrilled all at once. Instead, her expression was of mild confusion combined with tolerant amusement.

"Should I know him?" she asked.

"The guy who founded Transtar?" Pat offered.

Nadia slowly shook her head.

"He makes those wearable smartphone-glasses combos?" Pat said, sounding increasingly desperate. "He funds Titan Or Bust! He's on StarTalk with…" Seeing her continued lack of comprehension, he sighed and looked dejected. "He's a genius, and he's getting interviewed by yours truly. This is super cool!"

Nadia chortled, then reached out and ruffled Pat's shaggy brown hair. "I'm glad, Pat." She sighed, then drew herself up. "I can't wait to read all about it." She then focused, and Pat could see her professional mask slip over her face. It wasn't a real mask, of course. It was a subtle shift in her attitude, her posture, how she talked. Even her accent changed slightly, downplaying her Scottish upbringing for a more posh London cadence. All of it turned her from his Nadia into Nightshade; into something different. Not something bad.

Not bad in the slightest.

She kissed Pat goodbye and he watched her go out the door. He sighed quietly. "How the hell did I snag a goddess like her?" he muttered to himself. Then he grabbed his phone, which he had recently loaded up with a dictation program for the interview. His eyes settled on the notepad and pencil he had used in the desperate, scrambling climb from 'wannabe writer' to 'struggling writer.' He grinned, shaking his head. "Don't wanna be a Luddite, do I?"

He turned, leaving the pad and pencil on the table, as he exited the door.

* * *

"I was excited for what would happen that day. But life had additional plans for me."

* * *

The old anteater didn't seem to know that there were other people on the sidewalk as she puttered by on a mobility scooter. Her eyes were covered by glasses so thick they made her seem to have no whites, and the small wireframe cart attached to the handlebars of the scooter was overflowing with bags of groceries. The sidewalk provided a rattling progress for her, and that sound was what caused Pat to look up from checking his maps app for the location of the interview, just in time to see the scooter rush right at him. He yelped and sprang aside, but the side of the wire cart struck his elbow. Both his phone and a bag of groceries went flying through the air.

Pat opened his mouth, his entire body freezing, his tail sticking straight out behind him.

The phone spun through the air.

Landed.

Right on one of the grocery bags that had fallen from the cart, which cushioned it nicely.

Pat blew out an explosive sigh.

"Oh deary me," the anteater cooed, reaching down and groping around for the bag. "Who put a wall there?"

She grabbed the bag. The phone skittered off into the street, where it was promptly run over by a double-decker bus. Pat held it in his hands a few moments later, whimpering softly as he looked at the crumpled, ruined wreck. But the shock and horror was soon eclipsed by growing fear. He had to get to the interview. He had to *do* the interview!

"Fuck," Pat whispered, trying to pack away his feelings and think calmly. He turned and ran down the sidewalk, almost running into a lamp post, tripping on a crack in the street, hopping across a crosswalk while shaking his aching foot, then finding himself near a collection of shops. He saw one was a stationary store, and his heart soared. He ran towards the store and smacked into the glass door with a loud *slap*. He grunted, staggered backwards, then rubbed his forehead. "What the—"

A mouse girl wearing the shop's uniform paused as she walked past the door. She saw his look of confusion and sighed, clearly completely done with giving a shit for the day. She pointed at the paper sign that had been taped to the door: *Door Broken—go around to the side.* Pat blinked, rubbing his sore muzzle. He turned and walked around to the side of the store. There, he found a propped open door that led right into the glitter and sparkle supply section of the store.

Pat squared his shoulders and strode through, trying to not get distracted by the bright colors. He quickly came to the stationary and found the rows of notepads. Most were huge, clearly made for people who were interested in drawing. Another giraffe stood there, wearing a self-knitted cap, tongue sticking from the corner of his mouth as he eyed the pads. Pat smiled.

"Uh, 'scuse me, need to get to the smaller pads," he said.

"Oh, they're out," the other giraffe said.

Pat froze. "What?"

"Yeah, apparently an entire class cleared them out. Something about the teachers being rather draconian about phones," the giraffe said, biting his lower lip as he looked at the pads. "Do you think I should go for the cream paper or the white paper?"

Pat looked at the two pieces of paper. They were both white.

You have, like, thirty minutes to get to the interview! His inner voice screeched. Pat grabbed the smallest drawing pad left—which was still big enough to take a portrait on—then grabbed a collection of drafting pencils. He turned and ran to the front of the store and slapped down the pad and pencils on the counter. He hurriedly swiped his card—then swiped it again when the scanner failed. The bored-looking mouse who was working the register slowly looked down at the reader, then frowned.

"Try it again?" she asked lazily.

Pat swiped the card, growing increasingly terrified. He didn't have paper money!

"Oh yeah," the mouse said, rubbing one of her large ears. "Use the chip reader."

Pat choked back a scream.

* * *

With the too-large notepad tucked under one arm and pencils held tightly in hand, Pat tried to remember the route to the interview location. He walked about a block, each step reminding him how little time he had to get there, before he finally stopped and closed his eyes. He gritted his teeth, turned, and asked the first person he saw: "Do you know where the Royal Buck Golf Club is?"

An old-looking boar pointed and spoke in an accent so broad, thick and painfully English that Pat was barely able to understand it. Not for the first time, part of him regretted being raised in America until a happy chance brought him to London a few years ago, and subsequently into Nadia's life. His left ear twitched and he saw the area the man was pointing towards, and hoped it was the right way. He nodded his head in thanks and then started to jog off. He darted past other pedestrians, evaded getting doused in water by a bus splashing through a puddle, and finally came—panting, gasping, and quivering—to the front door of the Royal Buck Golf Club. The broad expanse of green that had been claimed near the edge of the city was bounded by a short wall and high trees, but he could hear the faint *twock* of golf clubs.

Staggering into the club's main building, Pat looked around with wild eyes, sure that he wouldn't be on time.

But there, right above the mantelpiece behind the beautifully varnished, wooden front desk, was a clock that showed the time with a golden, filigreed arm, aimed right before 12. He was on time. Then his eyes fell on Ezra Maes, and he breathed in quickly, trying to stand up and look professional and not like a goofy giraffe who had walked into doors, sprinted down streets, tripped over his own feet, and generally been utterly disarrayed from the instant he stepped out of his flat. Yet he still felt utterly shabby next to Ezra.

Ezra Maes was a buck, a male deer. His antlers were pared down to an elegant V, rather than sprawling in every direction like some bucks that Pat had seen. He was tall and broad-shouldered, his muscles straining against his sleek vest and rolled up shirt sleeves. He looked utterly put together and confident. He wasn't a man who had just surged out of bed and rushed about wildly; his buttons were polished, his trousers perfectly creased. He even had a tie that tucked neatly into his waistcoat . He was speaking to the woman behind the desk, his voice deep and rich—even if distance made his words indistinct. Whatever he said made the cute doe behind the desk go from bay-colored to pure red. She started to titter as Ezra looked at Pat.

He grinned brightly, holding out a single nimble-looking hand to Pat. "Patrick, right?" he asked.

"That's the name," Pat said, trying to match his casual coolness. "It's a pleas...er...an hon...um, it's *good* to meet you, Mr. Maes!" He beamed. "I saw the last ToB launch! Those gyrojets are freaking—like, wow." He shook his head, then stopped himself, realizing that he was supposed to be interviewing this guy, not nerding out about his privately-funded space program. But with that, Ezra's face brightened, his golden eyes practically glowing. He drew Pat closer, squeezing his hand and reaching back to slap Pat's shoulder.

"I think," he said. "We're going to get along *famously.*"

CHAPTER 2

"The first thing anyone notices about him was that he did nothing by half measure—not in his personal life, nor in his public attitude."

Twock!

The golf ball went sailing away at near-escape velocity, vanishing among a copse of trees that seemed to be clustered around hole three. As it flew off, Ezra—he had immediately asked for Pat to call him nothing else—set his golf club against his shoulder like some kind of cocky big game hunter. He grinned and looked at Pat.

"No, see," he said. "Enterprise wasn't a *bad* show. It was a *tragedy* of a show. Unlike Voyager."

Pat scribbled a few more notes. The huge notepad he had bought was awkward to hold, doubly so when Ezra's topics ranged far and wide. Since hole one, he had talked about Star Trek, the future of genetic engineering, the extinction of the lizard kind, lab-grown meat, more Star Trek, combating climate change with a very large mirror ("It would, of course, be in space!"), the dangers of technocratic oligarchies ("Yes, I know, guilty as charged!"), the latest round of negotiations with his union ("I'd rather debate with my workers than take advantage of them."), and, when he had time, even more Star Trek.

Pat took one of the draft pencils away from his notes. He had written in shorthand for years, but using dictation software had almost chased every last memory of how to do it from his head. However, the stress of both asking questions and keeping up with Ezra's excited stream of responses, tangents and at least three entirely new ideas for corporations that would usher in some new innovation to the world, had brought back his old instincts. He was surprised that he could actually read the tiny scribbles he had left behind.

"But the essential concept is sound. I've been thinking of putting my findings into the Light Seed project. Ever heard of that?" Ezra asked, walking purposefully across the grass. He moved with quick, bounding strides, his golf clubs bouncing against his back. He disdained a caddie and a golf cart, having dismissed the very idea as being utterly beneath him. Thankfully it wasn't a terribly long walk. When Pat scribbled down the last few notes, he looked up at Ezra and started to follow.

"It's that project to launch a small drone with a solar sail, right?" he asked.

"Should reach Alpha Centauri by the end of my lifetime," Ezra said. "If it's launched within the month. Accelerated by laser light up to, eh, point-oh-four C? It'd be the fastest thing that we've ever launched from this globe." He beamed. "That alone almost makes it worth the money spent. But I'm not exactly about *speed*."

Pat laughed. "More of an endurance man?" he asked, tail swishing behind him.

"Exactly!" Ezra said. "It's no sense getting there first if you can't do much afterwards." He licked his muzzle, then grinned as they came to the copse of trees. The golf ball was nestled in the grass, about twenty feet away from the hole. The cervine's eyes glowed with delight as he looked at the ball, kneeling down and drawing a line with his eyes from the ball to the hole. "It was Voyager—" It took Pat a few moments to realize he was back on Star Trek. "—that gave me the idea for the solar sail. One of their episodes had them building a solar sail capable craft. I saw it when I was quite young, and I became fascinated with the concept. I always loved tall ships. Ever read Patrick O'Brian?"

Pat shrugged one shoulder. "No…"

"And you call yourself a Briton!" Ezra sprang to his feet. "It's all about the time our fair isles stood up to Napoleon's tyrannical influence."

"Well, I was raised in America for the most part, hence my lack of accent," Pat said, then shook his head. He had gotten so used to Ezra's bounding topic shifts that he had almost forgotten he was here to interview him. "But, sir, two questions. If it was solar sails that got you interested in space, why didn't you fund a solar sail from the start?"

"Hah!" Ezra grinned. "I did the math, and I realized that Mars was a better choice for the first step. Then I did more math, and it turns out Mars is bloody *awful*. There's no magnetosphere, and the iron core is dead. Do you know what happens to an atmosphere without a magnetosphere?" He clucked his tongue. "Nothing good. So, I did more research, and it turns out the most Earth-like planet? It's Venus." He paused. "If you ignore the atmosphere. After *that*, though? Titan, one of the moons of Saturn. Hence, Titan or Bust. But your second question?" He stood, then placed the club against the ground, readying to take his swing. As he pulled back, Pat scribbled some notes, then grinned shyly.

"That episode with the solar sail…" he said. "Did you know it was actually from Deep Space 9?"

The golf ball landed five feet from the hole.

"Well, bugger me," Ezra said, his voice bemused. "That leads me to think—did you know there's a psychological quirk that makes people become more convinced of a fact that is incorrect *after* it's pointed out that it's wrong? Essentially, correcting people makes them more entrenched?" He shook his head. "Which is a big reason why…"

And with that, Ezra was off, bounding across more topics and ideas. Pat's wrist was starting to cramp.

⁜ ⁜ ⁜

"The interview was a complete success. Everything he did was a success, so it wasn't a surprise, really. But it was the meeting afterwards that shocked me."

* * *

"And then," Pat said, grinning as he leaned back in the comfortable chair in Ezra's office, "Vicky set us up and, well… we hit it off."

"With a *predator* of all things?" Ezra asked, holding a small, crystalline glass that he had filled with something that looked like whiskey but fizzled like soda. "Very brave." He grinned wickedly as he tilted his head back and downed the drink.

"It was a fight between her hotness and my terror, and… well…" Pat shook his head, feeling slightly chagrined at sharing the story, even while leaving out the clothes-ripping details.

The interview had ended with Ezra showing off a few gizmos and gadgets. Now, the pad was filled with notes for half a biography, and Pat was already starting to dread the future task of taking the wild rambles and condensing it into something readable and entertaining. But that was a job for future Pat.

For right now, Ezra had offered to give him a chance to sit and enjoy some drinks. The conversation had slipped almost immediately to the thing most often on the minds of the young and ambitious—levels of wealth notwithstanding.

Girls.

"You ever had a girlfriend?" Pat asked.

Ezra set down the glass. "No," he said. "Too busy!" He beamed. "But I've had a few friends-with-benefits over time. There was Ava in secondary school—ah, high school for you." He nodded to Pat. "There was Shelia in college. And her roommate, Morgan. And Trisha, Yolanda, Samantha…" He leaned back, his voice so confident and assured that Pat couldn't even imagine he was lying. "And then after graduation, when I was working at my first company, there was the CEO of a rival company, Marisa, oh she was *amazing*. Married, but amazing…" Ezra grinned at Pat. "We're off the record, right?"

Pat stood there, his face feeling oddly hot. He nodded meekly.

"Good!" Ezra said, chuckling. "I mean, she divorced her husband a week later, so I'm *fairly* certain their relationship was already on the rocks. But…" He paused. "I was kind of young and stupid. So, I told myself, no more taken girls. But after Marisa, there was another girl named Trisha. But see, the first one was this cute mare, she had a white star around her left eye, just *adorable*. The other Trisha I mentioned earlier was a mouse, the most flexible mouse you could imagine. Kinda had to be. If you know what I mean…"

Pat was not entirely sure he did. He shifted slightly in his chair, trying to find his voice.

A knock came at the door, saving him. The petite doe from before stuck her muzzle in. "Mr. Maes, a Miss Armitage is at the front door, asking where her boyfriend has gotten to." She sounded faintly amused.

Ezra blinked. "Oh! I'm a complete fool!" He sprang to his feet. "I've been keeping you."

"How long has it been?" Pat asked, then started. "My phone! It got—"

"Crushed, I remember," Ezra said, nodding as they walked out together. As they entered the lobby, Pat saw Nadia standing beside the counter, her workplace mien still settled on her face. Everything about her screamed *worship me,* even with the thick black coat she wore while commuting. She looked down at the deer lass who was working at the desk, and the doe looked somewhere between terrified and aroused as she stammered.

"M-Mr. Maes is—"

"Right here," Ezra said, stepping forward. "Miss Armitage, please forgive me for so occupying your paramour's time." He smiled, holding out one of his hands.

Nadia turned and her eyes almost glowed as she looked at him. Pat tried to imagine what she saw—or more accurately, *how* she saw. Ezra's boundless energy became a confident, almost dominant force of personality. His sleek, yet muscled form became something fast and graceful. From the look that Nadia sent—eyes flicking from antlers to hooves—everything about him was appealing to her.

"I was wondering where he'd got to. He wasn't answering his phone," she murmured, extending her hand, which Ezra took and gingerly kissed.

"It was crushed by a bus, I hear," Ezra said, grinning broadly. "And I suppose I must take it as a compliment that I was so diverting that he could spend a moment away from you." His eyes did the same to Nadia as hers had done to him. Nadia shifted her shoulders slightly, letting her coat fall ever so slightly open, teasing the buck with the ample swell of her breasts. And yet, unlike so many things she did, the faintly uncertain air on her face made it clear that it had been more instinct and whim than calculation.

And that only got Patrick more…

More…

He wasn't sure what he felt. A combination of sick fascination and intense need. A need all the more ferocious for the fact he had to restrain himself. Though every nerve in his body wanted to grab Nadia and just… fuck her right there on the desk, he had to hold back.

"Well, I'm glad he's had a good time being in your company, though judging by our brief meeting, I'm not surprised," Nadia said, her voice a purr. She took Pat by the arm. "See you later, *Mister* Maes."

She put a definite emphasis on the 'mister' and giggled as she took Pat to the door.

* * *

"Needless to say, there were repercussions."

* * *

"Ah! Ah! *Hnnn*—" Nadia's quiet, eager vocalizations broke off in a growl, her nails digging into Pat's muscular shoulders, her hips slamming against his as she rode him, the bed squeaking and creaking under them. She gasped and hung her head forward, her long, straight hair spilling down around her face, shrouding it slightly. Pat had been expecting sex, but hadn't been quite expecting this ferocity. As soon as they got home she had jumped into his arms, madly kissing him and tearing his clothes off. It reminded him of their first time. Nadia leaned over him and bit down on Pat's neck as her nails tightened on his chest. Patrick tried to summon up the...

He couldn't find the right word. His mind felt muddled and confused as her pussy slammed down onto his dick, making his voice come out in quick, gasping pants. He clenched his hands, his wrists restrained by bondage cuffs attached to the bed's headboard. While Pat wasn't into the whips and chains aspect of BDSM, he enjoyed a little restraint play, especially since it let Nadia indulge in her dominant instincts. He was like a captured prey, and it drove her wild. It pleased him to see her indulge.

He tugged at the restraints as his body flexed from her love bites. This seemed to excite Nadia more, seeing her prey struggle. She shuddered atop him, her sex clenching on his member as her teeth tightened. But while she didn't quite draw blood, the pressure was still enough to send Pat over the edge. He grunted and felt his cock spurting inside her again and again.

Then he went limp. His eyes closed and he panted quietly. "Jesus, Nadia..."

"Mmm..." She growled softly as she slowly laid down on top of him. She undid his bonds and licked his sore wrists before settling into a comfy position on his chest, her head crooked underneath his chin. Pat wondered if he had detected a faint tone of dissatisfaction in her voice. Her ferocity had seemed different this time, regardless of the bondage play. She was coaxed on by something else, and he had a feeling he knew what it was.

And that was when the idea occurred to him.

"So, uh," Pat said, feeling a hot, creeping feeling crawl along his scalp. His ossicones tingled and he felt his stomach do slow, casual flip flops. "Ezra and I hit it off pretty well. He actually invited me to chill with him again in the future."

Nadia nodded quietly, her nose rubbing against his spotted collarbone.

She smirked. "Should I be jealous?"

"No," Pat said, sounding wryly amused. His hand reached up, caressing her raven-black hair. Normally so neat, it was knocked askew by their lovemaking. His fingers drew straight lines through the strands, undoing tangles and producing a quiet, happy purr from Nadia. Quietly, Pat continued. "He, uh, was actually a bit of a player."

"Player?" Nadia asked, chuckling. Pat grinned, feeling like a total dork.

"Y-Yeah. He rattled off a list as long as my arm when I asked him if he ever had a girlfriend," Pat said, shaking his head. "And, well… you two seemed to…" He coughed as Nadia abruptly turned her head up, looking at him square on. Her brow furrowed and her tail twitched ever so slightly, lifting upwards, revealing some of her rump. Pat forced himself onward. "Well, I was thinking maybe that we'd like to try… stuff with him."

Nadia arched an eyebrow. "Stuff?"

"And things," Pat squeaked.

Nadia leaned her head downward. Her nose pressed against one of Pat's nipples, rubbing a slow circle against the hard nub. Her tongue darted out and she licked him casually, as if she was tasting his flavor. Then she grinned.

"So, you want him to fuck me, then?" she asked, shifting herself forward. Her wet sex glided along his belly, her hands pressing to his shoulders. She reared backwards, looking down her elegant nose at him. Her eyes flickered with a delightful glow that didn't seem to entirely be caused by the lamp light in the room. Her nails teased Pat with their sharpness. "You want to watch me get fucked by a rich, *powerful* man?"

Pat gulped slowly, his mouth feeling dry as a bone. His cock—so recently spent inside of her—was hard as iron.

"Yes…" he whispered.

Nadia smiled slightly. "Well, he must have made quite the impression. We can at least see where a conversation takes us."

Pat nodded quickly. And, with almost deliberate wickedness, Nadia slipped off him as she reached forward and undid the restraints attached to the headboard and tossed them to the ground, her ample breasts hanging in the air, obscuring his view. Soon her face returned to his vision and she kissed him softly on the lips before settling down and pressing to his side. Her thigh hooked over his legs as her hand slipped along his chest, caressing his short, bristling fur. She closed her eyes and quickly fell asleep.

Pat remained awake, reveling in a sensation that was as horrible as it was positively tantalizing. He wanted to reach down and cup his cock and stroke it and cum. But he didn't. Instead, he felt a melange of frustration and arousal; fear and excitement. It left him short of breath and achingly hard for what felt like an eternity.

Eventually, he too slipped off to sleep.

CHAPTER 3

*"I had expected our first conversation to be awkward. The only awkwardness
was in how quickly things progressed."*

* * *

Ezra stabbed a fork into the salad, then popped the contents into his muzzle. He chewed contemplatively as he looked from Patrick to Nightshade. Not Nadia. Nightshade.

And that was an important distinction. Patrick knew that Nadia put a lot of herself into her stage persona—and never quite took it all off even when she came home. For one thing, she routinely had her fur permanently dyed, so it wasn't like a costume she could take off when she came home. Even so, there was always a separation between the two personas, though it could sometimes be subtle. But Patrick always *knew* when he was dealing with Nadia and when he was dealing with Nightshade.

And God, Nightshade was something else. She was kitted out in an outfit that rode the fine line between her work clothes and something you could wear in public without being arrested: A low-cut clinging shirt that dipped between her breasts, making it quite clear that she wasn't wearing a bra. Complimenting it was a sleek skirt that suited the sudden heat wave that had rolled into London. Pat, meanwhile, was wearing essentially the same thing he had when they had last met—though less shabby and rumpled.

Ezra, meanwhile, was dressed in a white, button-down shirt and khaki pants that were nearly the same shade as his dark brown fur, giving Patrick a faint sense of sitting with a man who was going completely pants-less. His foot tapped as he listened to Nightshade finish the story.

"And by the time I was done," she said, smiling, "we were both completely late for the party and Pat had discovered a new... kink." Her eyes glittered.

Ezra grinned slowly. "You know," he said, drumming his darkly-furred fingertips on the tabletop, "when I was in secondary school, I was always picked on. One of the downsides of going to Wolfstone Preparatory Academy?" He grinned. "Well, it was called Wolfstone *Predatory* Academy for a reason. Lots of canines." He shook his head. "But it didn't help that I was a fat nerd with goofy antlers." He gestured to his finely-manicured appendages. "It wasn't until my third year there that I found my perfect means of revenge."

"And what was that?" Night purred.

Ezra picked up a glass. "My cock," he said, utterly casual.

They were in a restaurant; a fancy place that Pat could have never afforded, but Ezra had insisted on paying for all of them. Since Pat was too nervous to eat, he had waved off an entree and fumbled at the bread platter. Nightshade was simply waiting with a predator's patience for her steak. Pat looked around with wide eyes, terrified one of the daintily-dressed waiters or waitresses would have walked by to hear Ezra's comment. He could already imagine the looks. Nightshade leaned forward.

"Go on," she said.

A faint rustling sound drew Pat's attention. He subtly turned his head to the side and could see that one of Night's shoes had slipped from her foot. The foot in question was nowhere to be seen. Ezra grinned broadly—cockily, even.

"Well, I kept myself covered in the locker. I was a teenager. You know how self-conscious teenagers can be." He sighed, but the tone was happy. The faint rustling sound came to Pat's ears again and he felt himself go almost beet red. Even though his own cock wasn't being caressed by Night's foot, it was still hard enough that he was worried the zipper might break. Then Night's eyes widened and her jaw opened in shock.

Ezra, seeing that, smirked with the utter assurance of an alpha male.

"It took a bully yanking my shorts down for me to realize that I had *nothing* to be ashamed of."

Night's foot thumped against the ground, her leg clearly going completely nerveless.

"W-Well," she said, quietly.

"I fucked the girlfriends of the three worst bullies by the end of that week," Ezra said, shrugging one shoulder. Pat gulped loudly as Night looked on, her breath coming in short, soft pants. Her nipples were peeking through her low-cut shirt and she shifted her arms. Not to cover them, oh no. She was moving to make sure Ezra could see the impact he was having on her. "It was one part newly-gained confidence, one part rumor about my equipment, and... well, one part that they were dating total arseholes."

"And then you went to college and—"

"Got buff, then got rich," Ezra said, swirling his fork in his salad. "Well. *Richer*. I didn't go to a prep school because my parents were living on welfare. The only thing I didn't do myself was the acne—that just happened to clear out once puberty was done using me as a punching bag. Oh, and I started manicuring my antlers." He grinned. "I've managed to avoid fucking men's significant others... *most* of the time." He purred that last bit, his eyes glittering.

Night breathed out.

The waiter arrived with the steak and as Night started to pick up her silverware, Ezra looked at Pat. He smiled. "But, of course, they were arseholes, and *I* was an arsehole. Everyone's an arsehole when they're a teenager. It's a sad fact of life. But you're a good guy, Pat. I wouldn't want to do anything that makes you uncomfortable."

It was Night who squeezed Pat's shoulder. He glanced at her and saw her smile—encouraging, but so very eager. He couldn't possibly disappoint those hungry, shining eyes of hers. He squared his shoulders, coughed, then looked back at Ezra.

"W-Well, I won't lie," he said, picking up another chunk of bread from the platter. Rather than eating it, he tore it in half, as if he was going to butter it.. "I am... kinda..." He coughed.

"Turned on?" Ezra asked.

Even while being kind and forthright, he still managed to show up Pat.

The worst part was it made Pat's member pulse with eagerness at the thought of Ezra taking Night. And from the way she had reacted to touching his bulge, he had to be... he couldn't have been exaggerating. Pat had seen Night's toys—including that monstrous dildo she sometimes playfully threatened his ass with.

Pat nodded shyly.

Ezra smiled as Nightshade popped some steak into her mouth and chewed happily.

"So, we'll need to set boundaries. What are yours?" Ezra asked.

Nightshade swallowed. For just a moment, Pat saw a flicker of hesitation in her eyes. But then he felt decisiveness solidify in his gut. He slammed his palm onto the table and said: "None!"

Ezra looked amused. "None?"

"Pat, you don't want to overdo it right out of the gate," Night whispered, concerned.

"I trust you," Pat said, smiling at her. "I know you'll handle it. You're a pro, remember?"

"Former pro," Night mused. She turned to Ezra. "I think we should start simple and see where it goes from there." She looked at Pat with a slightly mischievous grin. "We'll plan our scenes carefully. Pat won't know what to expect. That'd ruin the surprise."

"Surprise, eh?" Ezra said slyly, arching an eyebrow.

"Oh indeed. I'm very good at surprises," Nightshade said, licking her lips. "One more thing. I don't do anal. That's off limits."

Pat whined. He worshipped that ass, but was never allowed to get inside it. Night had tried anal when she was younger, and didn't care for it. Since then, she'd had a strict 'no backdoor' policy. It drove Pat wild, and she knew it. They had a half-joking agreement that if she ever let Pat do her anally, she'd get to peg him in return. This didn't stop Pat from joking about it often.

Ezra leaned back in his chair. "Sounds reasonable. Otherwise, we've got a wide berth. Oh, and I should mention, I'm a top. That works well for my part as the 'bull,' but what about you, dear?"

"I can play the submissive. I've done it before," Nadia said. "It's not my *forte*, but I think it would be exciting to delve into. As a hobby." Her eyes glinted and she grinned as she stabbed her fork into a bit of steak, twirling it on the plate playfully.

"You, submissive? Now that's something I'd pay to see," Pat chuckled. Nightshade shot him a cold glance, but her face quickly softened. She placed her hand gently on Pat's thigh.

"You get it free, Pattycakes," she said. Then, grinning. "Save for when Glitter is involved."

"Glitter?" Ezra asked, arching an eyebrow at the two of them. He looked like he was trying to picture Night picking bits of glitter out of her fur. Night chortled, then picked her bit of steak up, swinging it into her mouth.

"My boss," she said, casually. "She used to be a dancer, like me. It's her nickname. She worked her way up to manager. She always makes Pat pay when he shows up at the Safari for my dances. No discounts for boyfriends."

"Ahhh," Ezra said, slowly. "*Now* it makes sense."

"Hmm?" Pat looked from Night to the burly stag. Ezra's grin was delighted.

"Oh, just, your confidence in letting your girlfriend get in some extra-curricular anatomical lessons," he said, in what was quite possibly the nerdiest way that Pat had ever heard 'getting some strange' phrased in his life. "You must not be the jealous type if you're supportive of seeing her perform for other men. In fact, you seem quite the opposite."

"Hey, if I wasn't enthusiastically supportive of her stripping, I'd be floating face down in the Thames right now!" Pat said, cheerfully, while Night slipped her hand from his shoulder to the broad back of his neck, slipping her hand to his throat and lightly pressing the sharp nail on her index finger against it. Her grin was predatory.

"Hmm, I think I'd rather eat you," she purred.

"Help me," Pat whispered, overdramatically. Night managed to look menacing for about two seconds before both of them cracked up. Ezra shook his head, slowly, and once Pat had wiped a single tear out of his eye, Ezra leaned forward.

"So. No limits…" His large finger drew slow circles on the table. "You in?"

Nadia's eyes—and it was definitely Nadia at this moment—caught Pat's. "Are you absolutely sure about this, Patty-Cakes?" Her fingers caressed him in slow, eager circles. He could feel her excitement through that touch, even if her voice was calm. But how much of that excitement was nerves? How much of this was scary to her? Pat felt slightly comforted by the thought that Nadia could have some nerves too.

Pat squared his shoulders and nodded, looking confidently at Ezra. But the instant he saw Ezra's wry smirk, he quickly scrambled to add: "O-Oh, also," he stammered nervously, "we should have a, uh, a way to stop it. If it gets to be too much."

"A safeword," Nadia and Ezra said at the same time. They both laughed and Ezra nodded, slowly rubbing his chin as he leaned back in his chair.

"How about *puzzle?*" he suggested. "That almost never comes up in sex, at least so far as I've noticed."

Pat and Nadia's eyes met. She looked amused.

"*Rutabaga,*" Nadia suggested.

"Rutabaga is a lot better," Pat added quickly, nodding.

"I'll admit I'd never think of bringing up a root vegetable during sex,"

Ezra chuckled, rubbing his chin. "So… when do we start all this?"

"Immediately," Pat blurted out, causing Nadia to scrape her knife on her plate while cutting the last part of her steak.

"Pat, I'm eating," Nadia said, popping a fresh piece of steak into her mouth to underline the fact.

"I don't mind starting early," Ezra said, deftly moving his chair over to be adjacent to Nadia. Pat's heart pounded in his chest as he wondered what would happen. Ezra glanced at Pat smugly out of the corner of his half-lidded eyes.

Nadia swallowed her food and put her silverware down. She quickly made for her glass of wine and took a sip. When she set the glass down, her eyes were glittering with a barely contained eagerness. It was Nightshade who cleared her throat and tossed her hair, running a clawed hand through the long strands with the grace and confidence of a queen. Pat noted how amazingly fast she could turn the flirt switch on. Years of practice at the Safari probably had honed her skills.

"I think it's fascinating you use another name when you perform," Ezra said, reaching over and touching Night's knee. She shivered at the touch, and Pat could see her nipples practically screaming against the fabric of her shirt, belying her cool demeanor. "Perhaps I could resurrect my old namesake as well."

"What was that?" Night asked, cooing.

"Buck."

"Buck?" Night laughed. "That's pretty on the—"

Pat noticed her abrupt pause was followed by her spine stiffening. The hand that was playing with her hair dropped to Pat's hand that was resting on the table, taking it in a firm grasp for support. Pat tensed. For just a second, he started trying to desperately remember how to do the Heimlich maneuver. Night's ears flicked back as she opened her mouth to let out a quiet gasp. Pat felt his tension ratchet up a few more notches. His eyes darted down and he saw that Ezra's hand was no longer on Night's knee.

Nor was it on her thigh.

His hand was buried between her legs. Her skirt was rumpled and her thighs had spread wantonly. Desperately. Her eyes went hooded and her jaw hung open slightly as she panted quietly. Pat had never seen Nightshade get reduced to a panting mess so *quickly* without the use of his tongue. Buck smirked and shifted his grip, and Night's jaw snapped shut to cut off a moan.

"No underwear. You risk leaving a mess," Ezra... no... Buck,said with a smirk. There was something subtle, yet utterly different about him. The way he sat, the look in his eyes, the tone of his voice. It reminded Pat of how Nadia could turn into Nightshade in an instant. Ezra wasn't kidding when he said he had a persona for sexual roleplay.

"G-God, Pat," Night breathed, bracing herself with the help of Pat's hand. Her other hand grasped her chair, her body tense and bent forward as Buck worked his magic.

Pat licked his lips. It didn't work. His mouth was drier than the Sahara. His heart felt like it was going nearly as fast as Night's was at the moment. A part of him hadn't thought that they'd *actually* go for it. But seeing another man finger his girlfriend—in public of all places—sent shocks of cold and heat through him. His cock ached and he could feel a sticky, wet spot of pre form in his underwear.

A small, screaming voice began to buzz in the back of his head, slightly clouding his perception. But then it crystallized when he turned to look at Night's face. She was... so mesmerizing. Seeing her there, the goddess that she was, being worshipped by a new follower made Pat's heart swell seemingly more than his cock. His admiring trance was broken by Night's panting growing louder, as she slowly ground her hips into Buck's hand.

"That's practically my whole fist in there," Buck purred, pushing his unseen digits further into Night. "If you can take that, you *might* be able to take my cock."

Night gritted her teeth and dug her nails into Pat's hand. It hurt, but the pain only mixed with the newly-discovered, delicious feelings that swirled in his brain. He briefly broke his studious gaze to make sure nobody was approaching. The coast was clear for now.

"You know I'm going to ruin her, don't you?"

Pat snapped his attention back to Buck, who was staring right at him. The look in his eyes was completely unlike Ezra's soft, disarming gaze. These eyes were cunning, demanding. He swallowed, his still-dry mouth providing only air to soothe his throat.

"I'm going to call the shots from here on out," Buck hummed, his shoulder moving faster, his forearm twisting. Night's legs were pressed tightly against him, trying vainly to resist his momentum. Her eyes were squeezed shut, her mouth agape, drooling. She looked pained, but hadn't truly tried to stop Buck. "When I want her, I'll have her. You'll only get whatever I let you have. Understood?"

Pat's lips moved, but his mouth couldn't form words.

"I said, *understood?*"

"Y-Yes," Pat whispered.

Night stifled a cry and threw her free hand down to grab Buck's forearm as her back bent, her head ducking forward. Her shoulders shuddered as she closed her eyes tightly, her whole body squirming. Her tail flopped from side to side on the inside of her chair. She dug her nails so hard into Pat's hand, it drew blood. Pat winced, but put his other arm around Night, holding her steady. Slowly, very slowly, her fingers released him as the orgasm drained from her, leaving her looking limp. Boneless.

"F-Fuck!" Night panted, a line of saliva dripping from her lip.

"Later," Buck grinned, and then slowly retracted his arm. Pat could hear a faint *schlop* sound, and saw Buck's hand reemerge, glistening with Night's pussy juices. The deer casually took Night's napkin off her lap and wiped his hand clean, before tossing the napkin into Pat's lap.

"Rutabaga," Ezra said.

Nadia's ears flicked and she looked up quizzically, her breathing still heavy as she rolled on her orgasmic high.

"Did you enjoy that, my dear?" Ezra asked, his tone encouraging, soothing; completely unlike Buck's.

'Y-Yes. Oh my God," Nadia breathed. She turned to look at Pat, the line of spit still dangling from her lip. She quickly wiped it off. "Are you okay, Patty-Cakes?" Before Pat could even open his mouth, she noticed the small bloody marks on his fist and gasped. "Pat! I'm so sorry," she said, cradling his hand and proceeding to lick it tenderly, like a mother tending to a pup.

"Ah, it's okay, I barely noticed it," Pat said, stroking her hair away from her cheek. "Honestly." He leaned forward and whispered in her ear. "I can't begin to tell you how hard I am. That was *incredible.*"

Nadia's emerald eyes flashed and a wicked grin came over her face as she licked his hand. "We'll take care of *that* when we get home," she purred.

Ezra smiled. "All right then," he said, pulling his chair out and standing up. "That was fun. We'll have to meet up soon." He paused and reached into his pocket, pulling out a brand new smartphone and setting it on the table. He grinned at Pat. "That's for you, since you lost yours." He looked over at Nadia, and then leaned forward to take her hand, kissing the top of it. "Nadia." He smiled, then turned and nodded. "Patrick."

With that, he left. As he walked away, Pat breathed out a quiet sigh.

Nadia let go of his hand.

"That was... really something," Pat said, staring ahead. With Ezra gone, he could relax and let his mind and body process all the events. "How are you, hon?"

Nadia took the time to slowly drag her finger along the rim of her plate, gathering up the juices and bits of steak she had missed earlier. She held the finger up, showing the accumulated moisture. "I'm... soaked," she purred, before popping her finger into her mouth and sucking it clean.

Pat perked up, but before he could place his palm on Nadia's thigh, the new phone buzzed and a text arrived from a number that had already been saved to the contact list. The name was BUCK. And the caller ID image was that of a dick. Even soft, it was the biggest that Pat had ever seen, laying across a pair of furred, white balls. Pat's eyes widened as he read the words, and he could practically hear Ezra's voice purring them into his ear.

The bitch's mine all month. Don't touch her, limp dick.

Pat whimpered, but he wasn't sure if it was in purest pleasure or utter despair.

Nadia lifted her hand to signal a waiter. A buxom ferret girl walked over, wearing a dress uniform. Her voice was cheery—unaware that Nadia was still buzzing from an orgasm. "Can we have the check please?" the jackal asked.

The waitress blinked. "Oh, this whole meal was paid for by the, uh, your friend." She looked a bit uncertain—but her nervous expression melted into a huge smile as she said: "And can you tell him thank you? That tip was... it was... I'm very glad he was so generous!" Her head bobbed.

Nadia grinned. "I'll be sure to tell him."

Her eyes met Pat's. The sickly-sweet emasculation that bloomed inside of him, starting at his gut and working outwards, felt multilayered. Not only was Buck bigger than him, not only was he more manly, he was also *richer*. And he'd just ordered Pat to not touch his girlfriend for a *month*.

It's going to be a long month, isn't it?

CHAPTER 4

"I might have complained out loud. Who wouldn't have? That's what would be expected. But deep in my heart, I was excited. More excited than I had ever been in my life. A wise man once said that hunger is the finest spice. The same is true of sex."

* * *

Nadia lay with her head on Pat's thigh, her eyes narrowing as she focused on the screen. Pat sat there, his thumb twitching on the controller, moving the dialog choice between the *goody two-shoes* option and the *being a dick for no good reason* option. They were on hour four of the latest RPG that he had picked up; a sequel to a fantastic game that he had played last year. Pat held the controller with one hand, while the other rested on Nadia's head. He badly wanted to stroke her ears, to pet her.

He loved petting Nadia. And more, Nadia loved being petted. It was one of the many dichotomies that kept their relationship thrumming. But the idea of touching her and then not sliding straight into fucking her was agonizing.

"You going to airlock him or not?" Nadia asked, her voice wry as she nuzzled against his thigh again. Pat laughed, shaking his head as he tried to focus on the game, his hand slowly settling down on the side of Nadia's head. He stroked her ear gently, his thumb caressing along the tip. Nadia made a quiet *shurr* noise in her throat. It was the sound of a very happy jackal. That should have made Pat a very happy giraffe. And on one level, it did.

"Should I?" he asked, flicking the choice back and forth, back and forth.

Nadia chuckled. "Well, he gave the drugs to those space pirates, but it was so that he could pay for his kid's space medicine. Now, I don't know about you, but I don't *exactly* want to kill someone just for being desperate enough to buy space medicine to stop space sickness from killing my space child." She smirked, rolling onto her back so she could look up at Pat from his lap. Her ears rumpled as they pressed against his left thigh, and she shifted and settled herself in place.

Pat looked down at her. He felt so many things at once, it was hard to keep track of them all, but at the moment, it was a simple happiness that she had actually been paying attention to the plot. He pressed the nobler option. As the characters moved through the next part of their dialogue, Pat leaned backwards and pressed his fingertip to Nadia's nose, rubbing it gently. She nipped at his fingertip. That made him think about sex. Again. Most things seemed to make him think about sex this week. His alarm clock awoke him with morning wood, Nadia waltzed past him to the shower and sex reeked from her body—not an actual smell, but a thought, a crackling energy.

He had been obedient and hadn't touched her.

Well, okay, he had totally touched her. Their lives weren't entirely consumed by rampant, wild fucking. At least, not after the first two months of their relationship, where Pat hadn't gone more than five minutes wearing pants. The casual times spent between work were filled by quiet moments like this. If they weren't playing games together—or, more accurately, having Nadia watch while Pat played—they were reading books, watching shows, going on jogs, or seeing the sights around London.

The day after the lunch meet, Nadia had called Ezra's office to make plans, and had talked with him for a half hour. An agonizingly long half hour. Pat didn't overhear specifically what they spoke about, but he could discern her flirtatious giggling. He was torn between pangs of jealousy and burning curiosity, wondering what they were planning, or how close they were becoming. Any questions Pat had about what was going to happen were answered with knowing smiles or blown kisses.

Over the next three days, even the most innocent hug, caress or snuggle session had a sexual undercurrent. Knowledge that letting his hands dip lower, that cupping Nadia's breasts, or even kissing her deeply, would be going against what Buck had said. *Buck.* Pat's throat dried as he remembered the image that had filled the screen of his new phone. He had occasionally glanced at it when alone, imagining lurid scenarios.

Nadia nuzzled his thigh as the scene on the game went from conversation to combat. Goons were rushing onto the screen, giving the player what the pros called a target rich environment.

"So, why are they bad again?" Pat asked after he realized that he had completely zoned out during one of the cutscenes.

Nadia chuckled. "They're thinly-veiled Nazi stand-ins," she said, quietly. "Not very well done, mind. Wolfenstein did it better."

"Duh-doy," Pat said, sticking his tongue out at her. "But Wolfenstein isn't an RPG."

"Sure it was!" Nadia said, turning her head and chomping down on his thigh with a vicious growl, her teeth pushing against his jeans. She grinned up at the noise that produced and purred against his leg. "If you kill five Nazis with a knife, you get a *better* knife. That's like leveling up."

Pat scoffed. She chomped down again. Harder this time. Pat squeaked and stammered: "O-Of course, Mistress!"

Nadia grinned, letting go of his thigh. "Good giraffe." She closed her eyes, not being particularly interested in the combat scene. Instead, she shifted so that she was mostly laying on his lap and curled slightly in on herself, enjoying the closeness. "Because you are good, you are allowed to pet me more."

Pat stuck his tongue out of the corner of his mouth in concentration as he tried to hold down the fire button, use the left analog stick, and pet Nadia all at the same time. Eventually, though, Pat got sick of dying. So instead, he paused the game indefinitely and went on to petting and caressing the jackal. She sighed happily as his fingers slipped along her cheeks, to her neck, her shoulders. Pat closed his eyes and felt the tiny nip of her teeth against his fingertips for a moment. But the quiet happiness got interrupted by a low gurgle from Pat's belly. He blinked, then smiled ruefully. "Think we should go out for dinner? I was thinking we could go somewhere nice. The editor loved the first half of the article I sent her. That's worth celebrating, right?"

"Mmmmaybe," Nadia drawled, rolling her head back as she thought. "I might want to be lazy and order out. Just cuddle up on your lap and let you pet me more. Maybe feed me too."

"That sounds good," Pat said. "Though, will you ever let me stand up to finish the rest of the article?"

Nadia laughed heartily. "Of course not."

"I thought you were a jackal, not a *cat*," Pat said. Nadia smiled at him, and looked for all the world like a cat who had gotten cream, canaries, boots, and a dragon's horde to finish.

Pat's new phone buzzed. Barely thinking, he pulled it out, expecting a text from the editor of the magazine, or maybe a text from a friend. Maybe even a call from his sister. Instead, he found himself nose-to-cock with Buck's member. Ezra's *nom de guerre* was bold and fierce above the picture of his dick, and the words that filled the screen made Pat's mouth drier than any desert and his cock harder than steel.

Be there in an hour to take your girl out for dinner. Be ready.

"So, if we're eating in-" Nadia started, standing up for the first time in hours. Her back popped as she stretched.

"E-Ez... Buck is coming," Pat said, his voice soft.

Nadia paused. "Buck?" She turned. "He messaged you?"

Pat showed her the phone. Her eyes widened and her mouth opened in a quiet O of shock, seeing the cock for the first time. Even feeling his member must've been different from having a picture of it, right there. Her eyes glittered and she bit her lip and stammered. "W-What should I wear?" She hesitantly tore her eyes from the phone and put her hands to her casual clothes. Nightshade would not be caught dead outside in a wrinkled, oversized tee. Even Nadia wouldn't dare.

"T-The d-" Pat stammered.

"You're right," Nadia nodded, her eyes glittering with delight as she quickly decided. "*The* dress."

Not just any dress.

It was a dress that she had worn when they had been getting ready to go to a dinner party some months ago. Playful dirty talk had led into an eager and frank narration by Nightshade of her publicly humiliating Pat by fucking a guest in front of the party attendees while berating his manliness. She had explained to him it was a kink called cuckolding, where a man enjoys seeing other men have sex with his woman, often while the woman demeans him. Pat had grown curious of the notion, but had ashamedly kept it to himself. That was, until Ezra came along. Now, Nightshade would wear that dress to this dinner date—the dress that started it all to the date where it was becoming real.

Nadia stopped and took Pat's hands in hers. She was shaking, nervously, excitedly. She looked up into his eyes, genuine concern gleaming in hers. She darted out her tongue briefly to lick her lips. "Pat, I... I'm going to feel strange not having you with me," she whispered. She moved her hands to his chest and felt his heartbeat. "If you get worried, at all, just call or text the safeword."

Pat smiled and put his hands on hers. "Hey, remember, I said you guys had no limits. I want you to have fun." He reached over and caressed Nadia's cheek.

Nadia threw her arms around Pat in a tight hug. "I love you Pat," she whispered.

"I love you too, sweetie," Pat replied, holding her close.

Nadia pressed her nose against his neck. The soft, slightly damp warmth only made the sharp prick of her teeth nipping at him more obvious. Pat laughed and rubbed at his neck as Nightshade drew away from him with a playful grin. "Now, I need to get ready for my well-hung gentleman caller." She purred.

Night turned and hurried off, leaving Pat holding the phone. For the life of him, Pat couldn't stop looking at that thick, slightly pink dick. It was lighter than his in color, but... well, it was hard to tell scale when it came to a photograph. Maybe it just looked bigger, but Pat knew he was lying to himself. Buck was definitely much bigger than him, that was the point. The question that Pat was struggling with was how... why...

Why did it feel so good to know that right now, Night was taking off her casual clothes and sliding on a pair of maroon panties, the lace frill tight around her rump—but she wasn't doing it for his sake. He could practically see the light curl of her short fur peeking around the tightness of that pair of panties. He could imagine the feel of his fingers, caressing the place where silk and fur met, the difference becoming almost immaterial. He closed his eyes and when he pictured it, it wasn't his own tan fingers tugging those panties down.

It was the dark, slender fingers of that alpha of a buck.

Pat whimpered low in his throat. A tiny, screaming voice in his brain told him to tap out *rutabaga,* to end this now. But a bigger, more intense part of him was aching as it strained against his pants. And so he passed the time it took Buck to drive to their flat, waiting.

Waiting.

* * *

"There was no turning back. Had I opened Pandora's box? Let the genie out of the bottle? I was about to find out."

* * *

Buck opened the door without so much as a knock or a ring of the bell. He strode in looking like he fucking owned the place. His suit was perfectly creased, a dark red tie wrapped around his broad neck, his antlers only adding to the effect as he stepped next to the sofa that was laid out before the TV. He looked down at Pat, and the giraffe saw the rich green eyes flick from his ossicones to his crotch. A sneer crossed Buck's face and he shook his head, muttering under his breath. "Pathetic…"

The door to the back opened and Nightshade emerged, looking utterly divine in that slinky black dress, her breasts sagging slightly against the filmy, black fabric that clung to her, making her look both clothed and nude all at once. A purse was looped around one shoulder, and she had even gone all out, adorning herself in jewelry. A gold chain necklace with a green emerald rested just above her ample cleavage, and a trio of golden bangles rested on both wrists, jangling softly as she reached up to caress her earrings. Her ears flipped up excitedly as she looked at Buck, who walked over to her, grabbed her by the hips, and kissed her.

The kiss had everything Pat would have wanted to give her—a fierce, rough masculinity, Buck's hands cupping and squeezing Night's ass, assured that she'd let him. And she did more than let him. She ground back against him, her eyes going hooded, then closing as their tongues played together. When he broke the kiss, she was left panting quietly.

"Ready to have some dinner, my lovely Nightshade?" Buck murmured, cupping her cheek, his thumb caressing her muzzle gently. Her tongue darted out, licking the tip of his thumb, but she wasn't tasting him, as she often did with Pat. That implied a kind of dominant, predatory edge. Rather, she was licking his thumb as if it were the tip of his dick, her eyes shining with a submissive glow that Pat had never seen before.

"You can't believe how much," she purred.

"Now, I believe you said the Rose Garden was a favorite of yours," Buck said, grinning. "Let's ditch this little pussy."

"A-Are you going to keep me updated on how it goes," Pat started, but Buck cut him off by shooting him a direct look. Their eyes met. Then, as Pat watched, unable to look away, Buck took Night's hand. Buck's dark green eyes didn't waver, didn't hesitate, didn't look away as he guided Night's palm to his crotch, forcing her to grope him. Night needed absolutely no encouragement to cup and fondle Buck's cock through his pants. She didn't even look at Pat, while Buck never broke eye contact with the giraffe. He smirked, then turned to the door, slapping Night's rump with one hand as they walked out. Pat gasped as they left, stunned to his very core.

He…

He had kind of hoped that the first full scene would be played out at the flat. In their bed. But no, Night was out, and he had no idea what was going to happen. His stomach churned and his cock ached. Pat couldn't help himself. He grabbed his pants, yanked the zipper down, and grabbed his dick. His hand clenched tightly and he pumped himself once, twice, hissing. "F-Fucking pussy!"

He breathed out the words, shame and eagerness burning in his muzzle as he shuddered and spent himself immediately. There was no build up—save for the three days of exquisite torture. But that didn't stop him from seeing white and going slack against the sofa, cum soaking his shirt, dripping down his thighs, puddling underneath him as he gasped and panted.

"Whoa…" Pat whispered.

Pat had once tried writing fiction. Never quite had the knack for it. He needed real things and real people to anchor what he wrote, even when he was doing a narrative. But as he worked hard on cleaning himself up and wiping down the sofa, his brain managed to picture a vivid narrative. But then again, he knew Nadia amazingly well. He could see her and Buck walking into the Rose Garden. He could see them taking their seat. He could picture them chatting, laughing. Buck would control the conversation—subtly, of course. He'd guide Nightshade to amusing topics.

Maybe he'd even start talking about Pat. A weakling. Not much of a man, huh?

Pat put one hand on his ossicones. He always thought they were cute. But there was something about how Buck had looked at his ossicones, and then tilted his head, drawing attention to his antlers.

That all you got? that look had said.

Pat was hard again, even as he tried to sit down at his computer and get to work. He tapped a few desultory sentences, trying to distill what he had learned about Titan and the difficulties of reaching the distant moon into something the only vaguely scientifically literate might understand. But his brain kept going back to that image. He could hear Buck's cool tones, talking about the women he'd fucked. Talking about Nightshade's beauty. God, she was beautiful. And he hadn't been inside her for what felt like years. Pat half-closed his eyes, leaning on his elbows, his tongue sticking out of the corner of his mouth.

He was aroused. But he was also scared. What if it stopped being a game? What if she started actually preferring Buck? Er, Ezra. Er. Whatever. He shook his head slightly, looking at the screen. His brow furrowed as he saw the last sentence he had written: *The moon Titan, discovered by Cuck astronomers in the 16th century...*

"You are *such* a fucking dork, Patrick," he muttered, deleting the sentence.

But what if she does? a quiet, screaming voice screeched from the depths of his brain. It came from the same place that kept him up at night, wondering how the fuck *a simple guy like him* had managed to keep a woman like Nadia this long.

"It's just a game," Pat whispered. "Just a sexy game. It turns me on. Like, I mean, I get all the *fun* of knowing Nightshade is having fun without..." He paused. "Without... actually fucking her, geez, Pat, *great* pep talk."

He's you, the screaming voice said. *He's you, only he has a huge dick, billions of dollars, a mega corporation or two to his name, and* actual *fucking antlers.*

Pat opened his mouth to respond to that; to scream to himself that he didn't care about antlers, he had *never* cared about antlers until Buck had made it a point of comparison. Then his phone started to rattle. He had set it beside his keyboard and the screen was face down. He reached towards it, feeling almost like he couldn't bear to turn it over, but his lust overrode him. He flipped it and felt that delicious and terrible spike of eagerness return as he saw the name.

Buck.

And the dick.

That... massive fucking cock.

But there was no text message. It was an actual call, with the green button appearing on the bottom of the touchscreen, begging for him to swipe and accept. Pat gulped, then slowly lifted the phone to his ear while looking at his computer screen, gazing at the few hundred words he had written since Night and Buck had left.

He tapped on the phone and the first thing he heard was a quiet, masculine breathing. It sounded like someone was jogging, but trying to not let the person on the other phone get drowned out by the panting. He also heard a low, faint *burr.*

And quietly.

Underneath both.

A soft, distinct...

Pap. Pap. Pap. Pap.

The sound of a pair of thick, furred balls slapping against Nightshade.

"Your girlfriend is *virgin* tight, pussy," Buck drawled. "Holy fuck… don't tell me you've never dicked her before," he laughed quietly, each 'hah' spiking adrenaline through Pat. He tried to respond, but found he couldn't get his tongue to work. It lolled out of the side of his mouth and his hand instinctively went to his crotch. "You're already touching yourself, aren't you?" came the wry voice over the line.

Buck's voice made Pat sit up and try to defend himself. "I-I've fucked her!"

"Even worse…" Buck said, his voice full of a sneer. "Hey, Night, tell him how it feels."

Pat could see them. Not on the phone, which was growing slowly hotter and hotter against his ear, as if he were pressing his cheek against Hell and smelling the lust and sulfur. But rather in his mind. They were in a bathroom—that was what that whirring sound was. Maybe at the Rose Garden. No, definitely. At some point during the dinner, Buck had driven Night so wild that she had insisted…

"Oh God!" Night whimpered, her voice sounding as if her eyes were unfocused, her mouth opening in a quiet, hanging gasp. She didn't sound dominant. She didn't sound on top. She sounded like she was barely holding on. "Oh Buck! *Buck*…" She didn't growl. She never *didn't* growl. Pat's hand stroked his own cock and shame boiled in his belly as he clenched his jaw.

"She begged me," Buck said, the phone clearly back against his head. Or… no… Pat could hear Night's eager, desperate moans, the slight echo of a voice speaking within a tiled room. He was on speaker phone. Pat's teeth ground against one another. Buck continued, his voice so fucking casual. He wasn't even trying, and Nightshade sounded like she had been reduced to a simpering wreck. Pat bet that she was supporting almost all of her weight on the sink, her breasts mashed against the ceramic, her nipples grinding slow circles against the cool, smooth surface. Her ass had to be jiggling against the impacts. Buck's other hand was gripping the base of her tail, holding her up by it. It had to hurt a little.

But from all the times that Night's teeth had chased a climax out of Pat, he knew that a little hurt only made the pleasure better.

"I was gonna just work her up and dump her on you, since you'd been such a good boy. But then she broke down after the appetizers. She had ordered the filet mignon and... mmm... what did you say, dear?" He grunted slightly, the soft *pap pap* of his balls accelerating as Night tried to speak around the pleasure coursing through her.

"I needed *real* meat! Ah! *Ah!*" She cried out, then became muffled.

"Chew on those," Buck said, his voice sneering.

"Mmmph!"

"I'll buy you new ones. Fuck!" Buck grunted, then paused, trying to get his voice under control—but it took him less than a second. "I'll get you a whole new fucking *ensemble.*"

Pat whimpered—his voice nearly exactly the same tone as Nightshade's. Buck...

Buck had just shoved Nightshade's panties into her mouth. He was using her panties—the panties that Pat had bought for her—as a makeshift gag. And from the muffled groaning that came over the phone and Buck's faint hiss, she was cumming. She was cumming with her muzzle full of Pat's birthday present to her, while another man's dick plunged into her tight, ebony sex again and again and again. And with every *again*, Pat's hand pumped from the tip of his dick to the bottom of the base. He gasped raggedly.

"Y-You asshole," he whispered.

"You're the one over there," Buck said, his voice darkly amused. "I'm the one here. And, pussy, Night told me about the strap on you're too chicken shit to let her use on you." He sounded amused. "Think she might like watching as *I* stretch you out instead?"

Pat squeaked, the phone almost dropping from his hand, but as he caught it again, his thumb slapped the speaker button. Buck's laughter filled the room. Deep, boisterous, and utterly contemptuous. As Pat looked down at the caller ID image—seeing the very dick that was fucking Night silly—Buck said: "Nah, Night's right. You're too much of a pussy even for me."

Pat gulped.

"Are you touching yourself?" Buck's voice had grown insistent, urgent. He was thrusting faster now. Pat's mind filled in the image. Those panties had to be shreds of silk, filling Night's mouth, her teeth having torn them to pieces. Her eyes rolling back into her head, her ears shooting straight back along her scalp, quivering as her tail twitched in Buck's steel hard grip. Her toenails had to be gouging marks into her high heels with how hard she was curling her toes in orgasm after orgasm.

"Y-Yes…" Pat whispered.

"Louder, I can't hear you over the sound of your girlfriend's *fifteenth* climax!" Buck snarled, his voice tightening more. He had to be getting close. Pat whimpered and then said, louder:

"Yes!"

"You don't get to cum until you say it," Buck snarled.

"S-say what?" Pat asked, desperate, his hand letting go of his dick as if it had become red hot. A thick dollop of pre cum spurted from his member, sliding down his shaft. His balls ached. They were nearly going blue. Pat closed his eyes tightly.

"You *know* what."

The words were final. Pat knew. Feeling both the pleasure and the pain, he grabbed his dick and groaned. "I'm a limp-dicked, little pussy," he whispered.

Then he came. He had thought, earlier, that he could never cum harder than when he was on the sofa. He had been wrong. Utterly, utterly wrong. The receding pressure that had come after he had given himself a short break crashed against his body as his whole spine seemed to curve into a C. A groan emerged from his mouth, so intense that it was nearly pained. His ossicones buzzed and his bones ached as he trembled and shuddered, spunk splashing against the screen of his computer, draping across his keyboard, splashing his chest, flecking his thighs. His balls twitched and spurted again and again, as if they knew they weren't going to be cumming inside of Nightshade for a long while and needed to get as much out as they could. Pat felt all conscious thought fade and merely wallowed in the moment.

He panted heavily, his chest rising, falling, rising, falling.

The phone was quiet. Buck had hung up.

A moment later, a chime rang from the phone. He had gotten a text from Nightshade. Her sultry smile greeted him from the contact ID photo he had taken of her earlier that week. Pat languidly lifted up his arm, then let it fall back to the armrest. Part of his brain knew that he'd have to clean up. A lot. He had cum on his screen of all places. And his keyboard. That was going to be a pain in the ass to clean. But for the moment, he was so spent, so utterly tuckered out, that the thought of doing anything—even something as simple as picking up his phone—struck him as far…

Far too much work.

But slowly, he felt strength return to him. He picked up the phone.

And there, just as he had half-expected, was a picture. It was of Nightshade's perfect ass, propped up from her bending over a sink. The view was angled low, so he could see the pipes under the sink past her thighs and calves. Her thighs were pressed together, forcing thick streams of white cum from her pussy to drip down her dark thighs. It was clear that, even after he had cum harder than he ever had before in his life...

Buck had cum more.

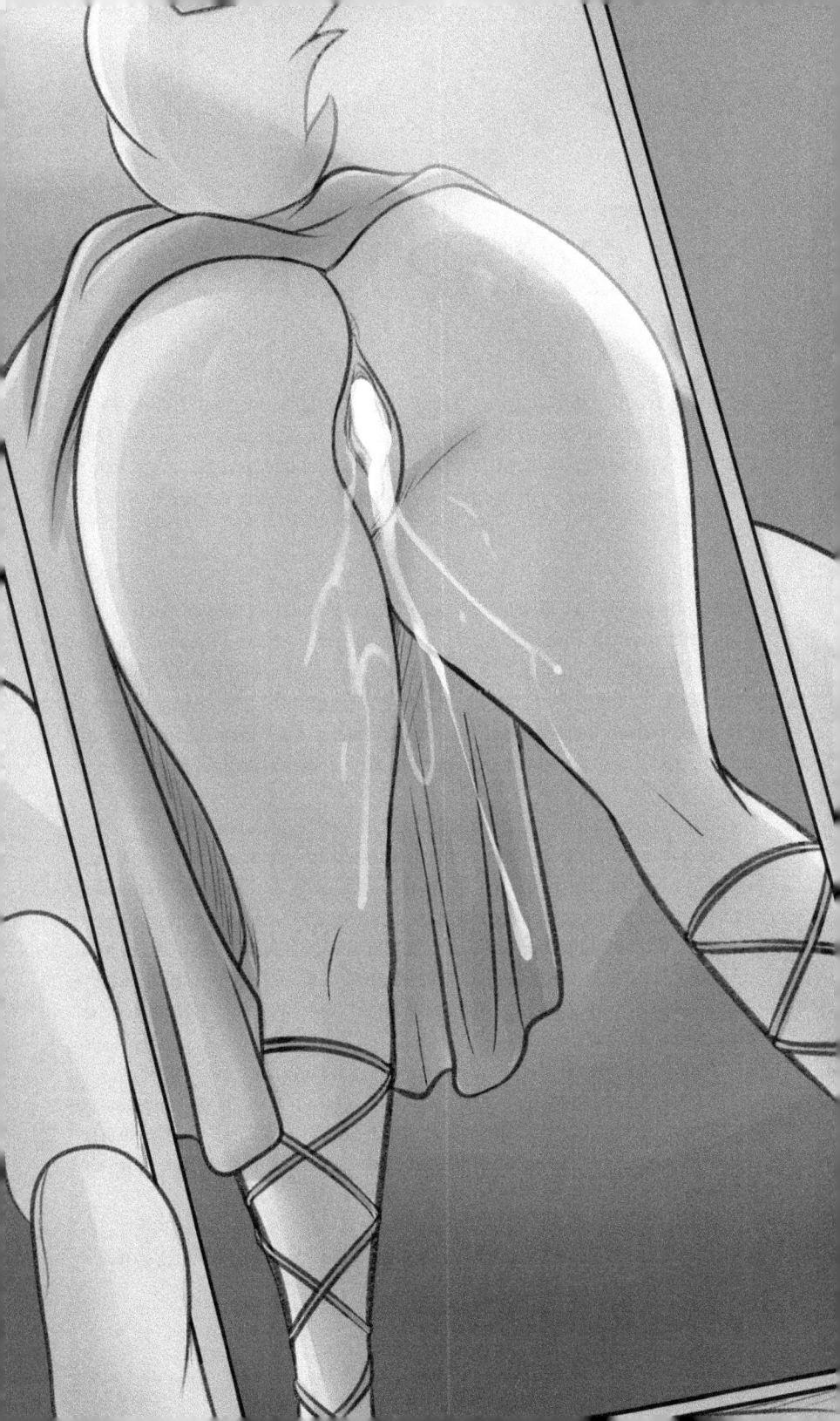

CHAPTER 5

"If you're reading this and wondering, 'How could he stand it?' Well, I'll be honest. I stood it because it drove me wild, and I loved seeing it drive her wild, too. That's all you really need to remember in times like this. But it got harder and harder as things got more intense. Yes. More intense."

* * *

Nadia showered Pat with kisses as he sat down at the table, his belly rumbling. Her muzzle bumped against his nose, his cheek and lips, making Pat want to blink a few times. His tongue met hers and they kissed and kissed. And kissed. Then Nadia broke away, panting quietly. She closed her eyes, pressing her forehead against his for a moment. Pat, not wanting to question a good thing, enjoyed her closeness. And this was after she had offered to cook, which was rare.

Though, fortunately, she was getting... better at it. Kind of.

It had been four days since the first date and Pat was not entirely sure what to make of the new normal. Buck had relaxed on the 'no touchy' rules, and Nadia and Pat had returned to their normal life. Which was ball-emptying sex followed by their day jobs, talking about their day jobs, relaxation time with movies, games walks and reading, as well as joking about the kinks they hadn't touched yet, like how much they wanted to do each other in the butt.

The fact it wasn't weird was what was weirding Pat out.

She had gone and fucked the uber-version of him, come home spent and happy as a clam, then they had cuddled and talked about the excitement of what had happened until they fell asleep. The next morning, she had woken him up with a blowjob. Normal stuff.

But...

But shouldn't something have changed? Pat felt that gnawing worry in the pit of his stomach even as he watched Nadia come back with the food she had prepared. She set it down with a flourish, grinning at him.

"See? You can teach an old jackal new tricks," she said, playfully. Pat licked his lips—the steamed, seasoned veggies smelled divine. He picked a carrot with his fingers, hissing as he tossed it from palm to palm before popping it into his mouth, freshly hot. Nadia put her hand over her muzzle, sighing loudly as she flicked her ears back. "Pat. We use silverware at the dinner table."

Pat grinned at her. "It smelled too good to wait!"

She sat down across from him and started to tuck into her meal. As she did so, she told him some stories of her day at the Safari. She told him about the other dancers, including her continuing rivalry with the insurgent star performer, Diamond—the wily zebra who was dating Pat's sister. Diamond and Nadia had never gotten along, which caused some issues with Pat getting to see his sibling. Nadia's eyes glowed brightly as she said: "And then I slid in after she fell on her stupid, striped *bum*. I took over the whole routine while she was being checked over."

"Oh gosh," Pat said. "Is she o-"

Nadia scowled at him.

"...out for... long?" Pat asked. "Cause if she is, that's good, 'cause you can continue to be better than... her."

Nadia smirked. "Nice save. But no, she didn't actually get hurt. Unfortunately. Though Vicky would likely make me cover her shifts, and that means I'd spend less time with you and..." She looked down at her plate and her voice became soft. "Um... I, uh, also got a package delivered to me at the Safari today."

"Oh?" Pat asked, sipping from his cup of lemonade. He wanted soda, but he had noticed a few extra pounds when he had gotten onto the scale. As he had said to Nadia at the time, the only thing he wanted to over-indulge in was her pussy, which had gotten her to leap out of the shower with the shower head in hand and the water set to maximum cold.

Nadia held up her right hand. A golden ring shaped like the eye of Ra glittered on her index finger. The symbol was tastefully done and not ostentatious. She bit her lip slightly. "Buck said he was looking for a cock ring for you, and wanted to see if it'd fit," she whispered. "Then when he saw how good it looked on me, he said I could keep it."

Pat flushed. Then, quietly, he whispered, his voice husky. "W-Well, ah... it suits you. I'd rather it stay there."

Nadia smiled at him, then tucked back into her own meal. She chewed for a bit. "Nothing to say beyond that?"

Pat tensed. His tail froze and his throat went dry as a bone. He picked up a cup, starting to sip from it—the water feeling less like a relief and more like him desperately trying to find a way to squirm out of having to respond to Nadia's inquiry. Even here, even at their table, Buck could reach in and smack Pat across the face with his dick. Pat's eyes flicked to the ring as Nadia's thumb caressed along the golden edge. Her eyes glittered with a pleased cruelty as Nightshade took over. "I'm kind of curious if it *would* fit."

Pat stammered. "I-I-"

"Mmm, I *did* cook. I should get a show..." Night crooned. She crooked her finger. "Up. Up. On those hooves, giraffe boy."

Pat sat there, frozen.

"Stand up," Nightshade demanded. "Or else I'll tell Buck you aren't following his orders." Her eyes glittered and Pat knew that Night could have—and would have—used her own presence to get him on his feet. But she knew that using Buck's name to goad him to stand was infinitely more delicious. Pat stood, feeling dizzy, his cock straining against his pants hard enough to hurt. He walked slowly around the table and Night caressed his pants, her hand soft, her eyes predatory. "Look at this *little* guy. I bet I could slide him in and barely notice." She paused. "Do you know how long it took for Buck to *fit* in me?"

Pat shook his head.

"Ten. Thrusts." She grinned. "Not gentle ones. Not 'oh, are you sure I'm not hurting you' thrusts." She cooed that last bit. Cooed it like she was talking to a baby. Pat squirmed. "No, he fucked me like a man. Hard. And fast. And he was so thick and long it was a fucking *struggle*." Her hand pressed to Pat's crotch and she tugged his pants down with a quick, efficient jerk of her fingers. Pat stood there, half naked, like a good little cuck, as Night breathed in his musk, her nose soft and wet against the base of his hard cock. She laughed, low and haughty, then drew her nose back. She held up her hand, comparing her ring to his dick.

"It'd fall right off," she said, sneering.

Pat knew it was utterly goddamn ridiculous. It was the tiny, screaming part of him that was trying to grab the reins back; the part of him that had briefly interrupted Night's roleplay fantasy months ago, where after she suggested a stranger at a party would fuck her, Pat suggested in insecure bravado he'd punch the guy in the face, much to her chagrin. But that was then, and this was now. Night and Buck had their hooks in him. He didn't open his mouth. He didn't even breathe. Night casually held his dick, pumping him—but with a bored, disappointed attitude.

She sighed as her hand worked him up and down, looking down at her meal. "It *is* lacking salt. That, at least, is something you're good for." She shook her head. "Salting meals. Cooking for me." She smirked. "Buck would never allow me to cook for him, you know?"

Pat whimpered, his balls twitching as Night angled his cock down slightly towards her meal. Pat's mind reeled. She couldn't possibly. Not. That. Right? Night's teeth flashed as she smirked up at him, those rich green eyes of hers piercing him. "Buck has *servants* for that."

Pat shuddered and felt his climax strike him with enough force to almost bring him to his knees. He had to grab onto the edge of the table, which creaked alarmingly as his balls clenched, and thick, hot cum spurted from the tip of his dick. With the casual expertise of a professional, Night aimed him and laid thick dollops of seed onto her meat, which glistened faintly with the warm, salty liquid. She licked her muzzle happily, letting go of his cock. Pat collapsed to his knees as Night sank her fork into the steak. She chewed happily, swallowed, then hummed quietly.

"I think Buck's would be better seasoning," she said, quietly. "But then again, he's more of a main course."

Pat gulped.

Night looked down at him. She waited, as if she expected him to speak. But Pat couldn't think of a single thing to say. He had cum hard, and the pang of humiliation mixed delightfully with the sheer joy in Night's eyes as she chewed on the steak she was eating. She licked her fork clean of some of his cum, then set it down. She had cleaned off the plate, and Pat's food had gone cold. At the moment, he was only hungry for one thing. But when he leaned forward towards her lap, Night put her finger on his muzzle, grinning quietly.

"Do you *really* think you'll eat me out better than Buck?" she asked.

"N-No..." Pat whispered, his voice husky. Wouldn't he? After all, Night had often told him there was no comparison to a giraffe tongue. In fact, she hadn't let him go down on her since Buck started to fuck her. Did Buck eat her out? What were cervine tongues even like?

Night sighed quietly, then shook her head. "What am I *ever* going to do with you, my limp-dicked little boy?" She grinned. "I could get the strap-on..." But at the look on his face, she chortled. "No. You'd like that

too much, I think." Her eyes glittered. "Do you think you can try and fuck me a tenth as hard as Buck can?"

Pat's cock, which had hung half-hard between his legs, sprang to full attention. There were some advantages to being in his early twenties. He leapt to his feet—but Night put her finger on his muzzle once more and shoved him back down with sheer force of personality. She stood, her eyes haughty, and looked down at him.

"First." She said. "Eat your dinner, and then clean up this mess."

Pat looked at the dishes, and the now-cold vegetables, then groaned quietly.

* * *

"Did you enjoy that, Patty-Cakes?" Nadia asked, eagerly watching as Pat quickly gobbled down the last portions of his meal. When he looked up, it was a warm smile and playful eyes that met his. He grinned, shakily. The intense emotions—the shame and lust, the humiliation and pleasure—slid off him like a thick mud bath, cleansing and filthy at the same time. He got up and walked over, knelt down and leaned into Nadia. She held him close and caressed his ossicones.

"Yeah," he said, when he felt like he could actually form words.

"Good," Nadia said. Pat started to stand, getting his hooves under him. He wobbled just a bit, his knees quivering. Nadia chuckled. "Need some help with the dishes?"

Pat gasped melodramatically. Nadia laughed and slapped his butt. "Will this be actual help, or sitting on the counter providing commentary?" Pat asked.

"That's help, in a sense. It's *moral* support," she said, then strode over to the island of the kitchen. She skipped up and landed, butt first, on the faux-marble of the central countertop. She kicked out her legs, then gestured to the washing machine that was set into the wall across from her. "I can advise on plate placement, direct you on what to rinse first, where to rack wet dishes."

Pat, who's knees were starting to feel considerably more solid, walked over to the kitchen, holding the plates in his hands. He set them in the sink, grabbed Nadia's hips, then dragged her to the side. The sleekness of the countertop made the movement nearly frictionless, and Nadia squeaked and laughed as Pat set her down, close enough for him to lean in and start nuzzling her neck where he then blew a raspberry—loud and reverberating.

"Ahh, noo!" Nadia laughed, then squealed again as Pat pushed her in front of the kitchen. "What's this?"

Pat slapped her butt gently. "I am exerting my masculine dominance," he said. "You get to rinse, I dry."

Nadia grinned. "Masculine *dominance?*"

Pat nodded. Nadia picked up the first plate. "Well, consider me put right into my place then, Mister Masculinity." She winked at him as she turned the faucet on. As she scrubbed the dishes, she murmured. "It's not too much, is it?"

"Hmm?" Pat asked, taking the dish she had finished and wiping it down.

"This thing with Buck… it's not going too far for you, is it?" Nadia asked.

"Nope!" Pat said, immediately. He didn't even quite know why. But as Nadia flashed him a smile, he figured it out. She looked so relieved. So happy. Her tail started wagging and she wiggled her hips a bit as she went back to scrubbing. Pat nodded. "Yeah, like, it's really hot. I love it." He grinned. "I'm not using my safeword for a reason here."

Nadia gave a little nod. "I'm glad, Patty-Cakes," she said, and went back to focusing on her cleaning. As she scrubbed, Pat thought over what he had said. It wasn't a *lie*. But why did it feel like he was keeping something from her? He wiped down another plate—and nearly dropped it when Nadia said: "So, once we're done, you're fucking me silly, right?"

* * *

"Yes! Yes! Yes! *Fuck* me, Patrick! Fuck me *hard!*"

Nadia's nails made a faint *creaking* sound as they dug into the head-board of the bed, which squeaked in time with the loud *pap pap pap* of Patrick's balls slapping against her belly. His hands clenched her hips and he slammed into her as hard and fast as he could. He almost worried about causing bruises, but Nadia growled with every thrust, grunting and whimpering quietly, her sex clenching on his shaft. She felt as wet and as eager as ever, and he felt her grip and squeeze him as she shuddered from her climax. Her voice was pitched low and vicious, a growl that made her words barely understandable. Pat was good at grasping her when she got

ferocious, and that just made it all the harder to keep himself from cumming right then and there.

"Yes! Oh *God* that hits the spot!" she moaned, her nails digging into
backboard, drawing thin lines of white. "Fuck me!" she grunted as Pat's
balls slapped her clit for the third time in the space of a sentence, the loud,
meaty noise of their hips meeting accentuating her words deliciously. "Ah!
Ah!" she gasped.

"God you're *tight*," Pat groaned, almost under his breath. "I'm shocked,
after going a, nnh, round with Buck!"

"Ahh, that's…ah, not how pussies work!" Nadia said, managing to
speak through the laughter and the moans of pleasure that burst from her
mouth. Her tail writhed against Pat's chest as she bucked her hips back
hard, the whole bed creaking. Her sex clenched on him as she wailed in
wordless bliss, her juices flowing around his cock, dripping down his balls.

Pat shuddered. He couldn't help himself. His hands squeezed Nadia's
hips as hard as possible and she hissed with pleasure as his balls clenched
and he spent himself inside her. Seed spurted into her sex, filling her
womb. It dripped past Pat's cock, slipping along his balls, puddling on the
bed underneath him. He panted heavily, almost collapsing into Nadia as
she sprawled underneath him, twitching. She had cum, and cum hard.
Quietly, she breathed.

"Oh *Pat…*"

Pat felt another twitching, shuddering wave of pleasure pulse through
his body at the tone of voice she used. It wasn't enough to set off another
spurt of cum, but it was enough to make him groan in the base of his
throat. His cock softened only slowly as Nadia panted underneath him.
She let herself lie down on the bed, her breasts pressing against the sheets.
Her head rested against her arms and she closed her eyes, moaning happily. She seemed even happier when Pat slid to the side and laid beside her.

"I know," he said, between pants.

"Hmm?" Nadia murmured, drawing herself next to him.

"About the pussies thing," Pat said, grinning. "You guys have *babies*.
Babies are always bigger than dongs. It's just dirty talk."

Nadia chuckled. "I was just making sure, with you Yanks and your piss
poor sex ed."

"Hey, *my* sexual education was top tier!" Pat said, grinning as Nadia
spread her fingers against his chest.

"I know. I taught you," Nadia said, grinning fiercely at him. Pat stuck his whole tongue out at her. She leaned in close, whispering into his ear, faux-secretively: "It's actually pretty hot. No matter *how* silly. Don't tell anyone." She slid her fingers along his chest, teasing his tuft of chest fur. Pat slid his arm around her back, drawing her closer, then reached up with his other hand, stroking her hair. Nadia closed her eyes and leaned against him more.

Pat let out a long, slow sigh. But rather than sounding completely happy and contented, it came out sounding more... wistful. Uncertain.

"You okay, Patty-Cakes?" Nadia murmured.

"I was just..." Pat paused. What *was* he thinking? After the heat and the passion had passed, he realized that a tiny part of his brain had been still been comparing himself to Buck. That was why he'd brought Buck up in the first place. He clicked his tongue. "I was just thinking about Buck fucking you and, uh, how...it...it's hot. Even when we're like this."

Nadia turned to look at him. Her eyes were soft. "That's why you're my wee, subby giraffe boy," she mused, giving his nose a lick. "But I'm happy you're having fun. I know I definitely am."

Pat grinned. "Would you say that Ezra is *bucking* your spirits?" He asked.

"That's not a pun," Nadia said, her voice flat.

Pat rolled onto his side, then started to rub her belly. Nadia crooned and stretched, opening more of her body up to Pat's touch. "The word you're looking for is compersion," she said as Pat stroked around her belly button with one finger. "The pleasure of seeing your lover enjoying themselves—even if you're not the one causing it."

Nadia reached up to cup Pat's cheek. "The best part about being with Buck is how it adds spice to *us*, Pat." She leaned forward, nipping at his neck and rolling him onto his back. Pat let himself lie back and enjoy the comfortable warmth of her body molding against his.

"I'm glad you're enjoying this," she whispered, beginning to drift off to sleep, "because I'm fucking him again as soon as he lets me..."

Pat breathed in quietly and laid there while Nadia nuzzled his neck as she slowly fell asleep. Her words rang in his ears—and his cock was hard as a rock again. He knew that even trying to jerk off again would be pushing his body past its endurance. But the desire kept him awake long into the night, thinking... thinking...

It was all just a game. Nadia loved him. She knew this got him off.

Did she?

Well, of course she did. She used to be a dominatrix. She knew how these things worked. And most of all, she knew *him*. She loved *him*.

How?

She was wearing another man's ring, after all.

Pat couldn't stop thinking about that—of how it made him feel. The faint buzz of the ceiling fan provided a soft white noise. He eventually did fall asleep.

But sleeping didn't help.

* * *

Pat looked around and found himself in a landscape that seemed to be a sea of darkness. Reddish, cloudy skies stretching endlessly into the horizon. No structures or people were in sight, but slowly in front of him arose the upper torso of an impossibly large, antlered creature. It towered high into the sky above him. Pat felt himself shrink smaller and smaller as a booming voice filled his ears.

Sick. Pervert. I can't believe you. You're into this? You pathetic little worm. If she leaves you, it's your own fault.

Nadia suddenly appeared beside him, she turned and glowered at Pat, her eyes disdainful.

Why would I want somebody as boring as you, when I can have him?

She turned away and walked straight towards the antlered beast, her hips swaying seductively, tail swishing luxuriously. She stretched out her arms, beckoning the creature, leaving Pat standing alone.

Yes, take me. Give me what I need. I'm tired of living a boring life with him. He's holding me back. He's pathetic. I need to return to my roots and live again. I need more!

The antlered beast roared in laughter as the world grew dark. Pat called out Nadia's name and reached out to her, but something pulled him back. Slowly he felt himself be pulled into a void as Nadia, ignoring him, continued walking towards the beast.

Soon, all Pat could hear was the booming echo of the beast's laughter, which was quickly joined by the pleasurable moans of Nadia. And then nothing. A great, yawning silence—and solitude.

* * *

Pat sat up, gasping, his eyes wide. Nadia mumbled under her breath, looking around, sitting up as well. The sun hadn't even started peeking through the window, but Nadia had rolled in her sleep to sprawl against Pat. She now nuzzled against him, sleepy and confused.

"Whazwrong?" she mumbled.

Pat, his heart racing a mile a minute, stammered.

"Nothing. N-Nothing at all."

They laid back down and Nadia snuggled him and drifted off to sleep again. Pat lay there and watched as the light grew brighter and brighter.

When Nadia woke again, she still laid beside him, nuzzling his chest gently. Silence remained hanging in the air, broken only by the distant city sounds and the buzz of their fan.

"You okay, Pat?" Nadia asked.

"Yeah," he said, softly.

She grunted, pushing herself so that her breasts mashed against his belly and her arms sprawled across his shoulders. Her emerald eyes met his in the early morning darkness and she flicked her ears back ever so slightly.

"Don't lie to me, Patrick," she said.

Pat gulped, then grinned. "Being cucked is… intense."

Nadia nodded. "Yes, it is." She frowned, and Pat could see that she was noting his uncertainty, compared to last night. "Did sleeping on it change your mind?"

"Well, I don't want to give it up. I… I really like it," Pat said—and he wasn't lying. He had never cum that hard before. But that screaming voice remained. He squashed it down. "It's… I dunno. It's like a drug. I find the conflict addicting."

Nadia smirked. "Well, yeah. But addiction isn't necessarily a good thing."

"Not even if I'm addicted to you?" Pat chuckled.

"Well, too much of me is hardly a bad thing," Nadia grinned in response.

"Heh, well, seeing you indulge…" Pat said. He felt his cock jump a little. "It's hot, but also scary. I think sometimes I worry you find me boring compared to your old lovers."

Nadia crossed her arms over Pat's chest and rested her chin on them. "Patty-Cakes, you're *all* I need."

"I know, but…" Pat stopped. "Really?"

Nadia nodded. "If I had too? I'd just be with you." She slid her arm around his neck, drawing in for a quick hug. She slid back, then put her hand on his shoulder. "I'd still *dance*, mind!"

"Oh, yeah," Pat said, nodding. "But, really? There's no part of you that misses your old life?"

Nadia's eyes shifted and she cocked her head. Pat suddenly wished he hadn't asked—he could see her weighing her opinions The next few seconds felt like agony. Nadia's eyes met Pat's. "I'll admit, sometimes… I do miss those days. But I was a different person back then. I'm honestly happier with you than I've ever been before." She grinned toothily, showing off her fangs. "Bonus points that you're having me indulge a bit now and again."

Pat reached over and ran his fingertips across Nadia's scalp. "I want you to be happy."

"You worry too much, Patty-Cakes," Nadia purred, leaning into his head-scratches.

"Maybe." He relished the feeling of her relaxing to his touch, her pleasure bringing him pleasure. "I *am* looking forward to what you and Buck do next."

"Well, tell me if it ever gets to be *too* much," Nadia said. She ducked her head forward, nosing at his nipple gently. "There are some people who abuse their subs. They ignore the signs. Ignore the safewords. Or pretend to not hear them. They keep playing the scene when the other person doesn't want to." She shook her head. "Those *fuckers*…" Her growl was accompanied by her nails digging into the sheets. "They don't deserve to hold a crop." She looked up at Pat, her eyes shining with anger—anger that softened to concern. "Whatever happens, don't let me become one of those, Pat. Even if you think you're doing it for my sake. You *have* to be honest with me. That's the only way this works."

Pat put his hand on hers. "I understand," he said. "I…" he tried to find the words for it. But he worked better with pencil and paper, with keyboard and word processor. So, instead, he finished: "I like it. Honestly, I do."

Nadia nodded. "I trust you." She laid her head down on his chest. "I trust you enough to get me out of bed on time," she murmured, nuzzling against him. Then, quietly, she started to softly snore as the warmth and cuddling put her back to sleep. Pat looked at the clock and watched the time click forward second by second, minute by minute. He was fine with it taking as long as needed. But, eventually, the sun rose and Nadia had to get out of bed. As she showered, Pat brushed his teeth, and then went to make breakfast. Once they had eaten, Nadia kissed Pat's cheek, slapped his butt, and was off.

Pat spent the next few hours wiling away at his computer. His work pattern was fairly simple: Write a few words, check Twitter, write a few more words, watch Youtube videos, write a few more words, check Twitter again. In the background, he had put on some music. The playlist ground through his songs and Nadia's songs with equal abandon, cycling into and out of the 70s, 80s, 90s and 'oughts. Pat grinned to himself as he thought: *They ought-ah come up with a better name than that!*

His mind filled with an image of Nadia putting her hand over her face and sighing. But she would be hiding amusement at his corny puns.

Would she? that quiet, screaming voice was back. *Would she put up with you when she has Buck?*

Pat scowled. "Shut up," he said, then typed a few more words. But that fear wouldn't go away, no matter how much Pat tried to get it out of his head. Then his phone buzzed. Nadia was calling. Pat picked up the phone, casually tossed it to his other hand, then put it to his ear, grinning. "Suuuuuup!"

"Hey Patty-Cakes," she said, her voice wry. "Did you toss your phone around like a total dork?"

"Maaaybe," Pat admitted.

Nadia chuckled. "So, I got a call from Buck." She paused. "He wants me to visit him at his office once I'm done at the Safari."

Pat's face tingled. "Sounds good," he said, his voice brightening. He pushed down his insecurities. He would not ruin this for Nadia. Mostly because she obviously loved it. His cock had surged immediately from soft to iron hard at the thought of how Buck had to have called her. He could practically hear the tones of that fucking deer. So cocky. So self-assured. And now Nadia was already thinking of him, he could tell. His tongue darted out, licking his lips. "When should I expect you home?"

"He, um, he said it wouldn't take long," Nadia said, her voice husky. "I... thanks. For finding him, Pat."

Pat felt that tiny, screaming voice fade into the background. He smiled and leaned on his elbows. "Hey, I'm a serious journalist. I do investigations. I find stuff. That's my *jobbo*."

"Jobbo is never going to be a thing, Pat," Nadia said, her amusement coming through despite a sudden burst of wind noise. She had to be walking outside. Pat grinned broadly.

"It will one day. Jobbo *will* be slang, it will-"

Nadia sighed and hung up. Pat leaned back and smiled at the ceiling. His hand dipped down and caressed his crotch for a moment, his cock slowly subsiding. He shook his head and went back to typing. The words flew off the keyboard, filling up the page. Soon, he had the third quarter of the interview typed up. He referred to some of his shorthands, and started to wonder about going into some of the tangents that Ezra had brought up. He paused, his finger resting near the shorthand about the giant space mirror that would help cool the planet.

Ezra. Buck.

The same person. Right?

Not... really. Pat couldn't imagine Buck ever talking about using a giant mirror to reflect sunlight and cool the Earth. But he also couldn't imagine Ezra snapping a shot of his own dick and rubbing it in his face.

"There's a story there..." Pat murmured to himself. He tapped his pencil against his paper, looking off into space, then started to scribble down titles. *What the Cuck?* he wrote. No. Too crude. His eraser squeaked as he rubbed it away, and he brushed off the shavings. He tapped the eraser against the paper again and again. He spun his chair around and looked at the room as it swirled around and around him, then stopped. His eyes came to rest on the door back to the bedroom and—thinking of Buck and Nadia—he stood and walked back there.

There was the drawer full of her panties. There was the closet full of her dresses. And there was the place she kept the jewelry she wasn't wearing at the moment. Pat rubbed his chin as he turned, walking away, then walking back. He grabbed and opened a drawer with a quick jerk. There was the *Stomach Pounder*, the immense dildo/strap-on combo that Nightshade loved to threaten his virgin ass with. Next to it, he saw one of her riding crops. He picked it up, brushing it through the air.

I use this, Nadia had said. *To fuck the system.*

Pat stuck his tongue out of the corner of his mouth, remembering the conversation. He hadn't known that Nadia was a dominatrix at first—but she had taught him quickly. Not just that she had been. But *why*. He smiled slightly.

"Fuck the system," he said, echoing her. Then slowly, his eyes widened. He charged back to his seat and sat down, cracking his knuckles, and pounded out a five hundred word introduction in a blur. As he finished up the last line, he glanced up and noticed that the time had gone from early to late afternoon. His brow furrowed and he picked up the phone to make sure he hadn't missed any calls. He hadn't. Pat chewed his lower lip. Disturbing Nightshade wasn't a good idea…

But his whole body tingled, from the tips of his ossicones to the bottoms of his hooves, at the idea of calling her and having Buck pick up. He tapped through his contacts, but Nadia's phone rang a few times before going to voicemail. His thumb hovered over Buck's number and he pressed it down a moment later. The massive dick filled the screen as it started to ring, and Pat quivered with exquisite discomfort as he put it to his ear.

"Yeah, what's up limp dick?" Buck asked, his voice slightly tight.

"Just, um, wondering when Nadia was getting home," Pat said, his voice already softer than he expected.

"Once she's done blowing me," Buck said. "She's been going to *town* on me, since she's so starved for real meat." He chuckled. "She told me that you tried fucking her yesterday and it was like getting finger banged. Apparently, she had to imagine I was there to even get off."

Pat gulped.

"Hey, you know what?" Buck laughed. "Get your pussy arse over here. I want you to watch."

"W-Watch?" Pat whimpered.

"Watch me cum on your girl's face," Buck purred.

And without a second thought, Pat was on his feet and out the door— the computer screen going black behind him, the file saved and backed up automatically. Pat was a writer. He knew to never leave that kind of thing to his own habit.

CHAPTER 6

"That's the thing about exploring. It always leads you to unexpected places. Not always pleasant ones. But, if you're lucky, you can find paradise."

* * *

"You want to talk to Mr. Maes?"

The doe sitting behind the desk set off tiny bells in Pat's head—bells he wanted to ignore. He didn't want to sit here and wonder why she looked so freaking familiar. He just wanted to rush up the stairs, get to Buck's office, and get his nose rubbed in about what a little cuck he was. The excitement of actually getting to watch was too much to bear. But Pat forced himself to deal as the girl behind the desk looked at her computer. She was an utterly adorable deer, shorter than Nightshade, with a faux hawk of bleached blond hair and a pair of magenta glasses. Matching hoop earrings hung from her ears, and…

"Wait, I know you!" Pat blurted out.

"What?" The girl looked at him.

"You were at the golf club!" he said. "What are you doing here?"

"Oh, I'm Ez…I'm Mr. Maes' secretary," she said, nodding. "My name is Lily, and that was his golf club."

Pat blinked. "He *owned* that golf club?"

"He, uh, bought it as part of a bet, yes," Lily said, nodding pertly. "Mr. Maes told me that he wasn't to be disturbed. He has a very important video call today with Mr. Moench. He's from NASA." Her eyes shone with a familiar light. Pat recognized it. It was the exact same expression he wore when he thought about Ezra Maes' work. Before Ezra had become Buck, and dominated his life, that is. Pat gulped.

"Well, he told me to come right over," he said, knowing he sounded pitiful.

Lily sighed. "Well, we can at least check on him." She stood up, brushing her hand along her sky blue shirt. She turned and walked out from behind the desk, picking up a tablet computer and holding it to her chest. "Come along." She turned and started for the stairs that led to the next level. Pat walked with her, his stomach roiling. He was so nervous and so excited that he barely noticed the fetching tightness of Lily's ass, or the way her teardrop-shaped tail flicked from side to side. Pat slowed down for a moment when he realized that his shoe was untied.

He knelt down, looking up to make sure Lily wasn't getting annoyed with him.

She hadn't noticed he had knelt. That was why she had taken another two steps, and why Pat could see right under her skirt to behold the pink fold of her sex, surrounded with pale white fur. Pat's mouth opened in shock and his tongue almost hit the stairs, before he surged to his feet and tried to not show anything on his face. Fortunately, Lily didn't look back until she came to the second level, where she gestured Pat forward.

"Mr. Maes' office is right here," she said, cheerily. "Let me just knock."

She knocked on the door and it swung open—clearly not latched.

Ezra Maes wasn't in.

Buck was.

Buck, the arrogant motherfucker, was sprawled in a comfortable office chair, his fingers laced behind his neck. His shirt was unbuttoned but still hung from his shoulders, showing his pale belly and dark shoulders. His muscles were firm enough that one could trace them with a tongue, and his pants were down around his ankles. And there, underneath his desk, was Nightshade. She was mostly dressed, as if she hadn't had time to get naked. She had wanted this so badly she had gotten on her knees. Her muzzle closed around the massive thickness of Buck's cock, his member half in her throat, half out in the open—but all of it glistening with her spittle. Her tongue lolled out of her mouth, sliding along the underside of his dick. Her straight bangs hung low over her eyes.

But even under a desk, and even with those bangs, Pat could see the wanton submissiveness in those eyes. When Night sucked him off, it was with a kind of arrogant assurance. She knew that she had her teeth near his most precious body part, and was utterly in control. But right now, her every thought was for bringing Buck pleasure. Pat breathed in raggedly, while Lily stood beside him, her ears perked up in shock, her mouth wide.

"Well?" Buck asserted. "Get in and shut the door."

Pat stepped forward.

Lily reached for the door.

"You too," Buck purred.

Lily whimpered and stepped inside, closing the door behind her. She clasped the tablet to her chest, her cheeks dark red and shining through her fur. She stood and watched with Pat as Night bobbed her head forward, then back, moving slowly, carefully. She was a pro at sucking cock, but it was clear that every bit of her skill was needed for this monster. And now that fact wasn't something Pat could avoid. He couldn't pretend that it was dirty talk and trick photography. Standing there, in the room, Pat couldn't escape from the fact that Buck was far bigger as he was. Twice as big, twice as thick. It was breathtaking. Pat hadn't realized how intense it would be, standing here, looking at the two of them. His cock strained against his pants as Buck smirked slowly, his hand cupping the back of Night's head, rumpling her perfect hairdo.

"So, pencil dick," Buck said, his voice casual, as if he actually was in a video call. "Lily here has wanted my cock ever since she met me. Right, Lily?"

Lily nodded quickly as if she were a bobble head, the reaction utterly instinctive. But to be fair, Pat figured that if Buck said anything to him in that tone of voice, he'd nod too. Hell, he knew that he would, because, well… His eyes settled on Night. She was struggling slightly, her muzzle opening wider. There was a tiny choking noise coming from her, a faint gag as she pushed forward. But what was remarkable, and alarming, was the look in her eyes. Gone was the sharp focus. Gone was the intent, the predatory angle that she always wore with Pat. Instead, her eyes had softened and hazed. She looked cock drunk and utterly submissive, her tongue lolling along the underside of Buck's dick. Her nose flared as she breathed through it, and quiet whimpers sounded from her as Buck caressed the back of her head.

And he didn't.

Even.

Look at her.

His eyes were settled on Pat's, and he spoke about other people. He was getting his cock sucked by a queen, and he was treating her like a servant—and she was liking it more than Pat hammering away at her as hard as he could.

"Lily still goes knickers-free. She hopes that I might bend her over one day and try again," Buck said, smirking. "But, heh, tell him what happened the last time I tried to fuck you?"

Lily blushed, holding up her tablet to cover her face, as if it would hide her embarrassment. Her voice was soft, coy. "I-It wouldn't fit."

Pat's eyes flicked from Lily to Nightshade. He could see it. Nightshade was bigger. Curvier. And she had worked her way up from, well, people like him to people like Buck. He could see through the underside of the desk as Night's hand cupped her own sex, rumpling her skirt. The slick sounds of her fingers burying themselves in her own pussy only adding to the music of sex.

"So, I'm thinking…" Buck purred, brushing one hand along his antler, as if he could get it to be smoother and more elegant by touching it. "You fuck Lily. Your dick is small enough." He shrugged one shoulder. "And Lily can spend the whole time imagining it's me."

Lily squeaked. Pat stammered.

"I can't!" he managed to get the words out after more than a few attempts.

"Did that sound like a request?" Buck asked, his voice serious.

Pat shook his head, mutely. But then he tried to speak again.

"Listen," Buck said, his hand grabbing onto Night's hair, squeezing tightly, then pulling her towards him. His cock slurped further into her throat, making her eyes roll backwards. Pat could only see her whites. She trembled as she came. Pat wasn't sure if it was the effortless domination, or the feeling of a real cock in her throat. He just knew that his resistance was crumbling watching her as Buck continued to speak. "I *own* your woman now. She wouldn't complain if I kicked you down the street and sent you home with your tail between your legs." He chuckled. "But right now, you can fulfill my employee's fantasy. I can use that pathetic little prick of yours to some end. And you can, for *once* in your pathetic life, taste some strange." He grinned slowly. "Don't make me kick your arse out of here, bitch."

Lily's hands shook as she set her tablet down. She didn't look at Pat—she couldn't tear her eyes from Buck—but her fingers were deft enough as they undid the buttons on her blouse. Pat felt like he was in a dream. There was no way this was real. But as he looked at Buck, he couldn't look away from those eyes either. Buck was smirking ever so slightly, his hand caressing one of Night's ears, stroking it in that way she loved. The very idea of saying no felt impossible. Pat's fingers went to the hem of his shirt. He hesitated again, then tugged it up over his head, trying to act confident. Sexy.

Instead, his shirt snagged on his ossicones. Pat breathed into the fabric and felt a flush of utter embarrassment filling his body. His ears heightened the sensation of being blinded—he could hear the faint *glug* of Nightshade's muzzle as she bobbed her head up and down on Buck's dick. But mostly, he could hear Lily's soft voice. She was whispering: "Come on, come on!"

Pat spent a few moments tugging frantically, almost tearing the shirt. Finally, it sprang free and he blinked slowly as he saw that Lily was already completely naked. The teardrop shape of her tail had lifted up, showing the soft, moist petals of her pale, white pussy lips. Her rump was round and tight. His eyes traveled slowly up along her back, looking at the pale brown fur that crested on her shoulders, at her cute, swept back ears. And then... at her face, at her muzzle and her pale eyes—focused entirely on Buck.

Lily wasn't whispering for Pat.

She barely knew he was there. She looked from Buck to Nightshade, who had gotten her mouth down to the base of Buck's dick with a quiet slurp. Night was pulling her head back and forth, bobbing faster and faster. Buck panted softly, his nostrils flaring as he squeezed Night's ear to show her just how much he was liking this. But his eyes were on Lily. He grinned slowly as Lily wiggled her butt from side to side, the faint jiggle in her cheeks as inviting as anything that Pat had ever seen. His nose flared and his worries about what Nightshade might think were fading by the moment.

After all, Buck had ordered him.

"You ready for me?" Buck asked, his voice pitched for Lily.

"Yes, Mr. Maes," Lily said.

"Just Buck," he replied, somewhat sternly. "That's what I'm going by here."

"Oh... y-yes sir, Buck, sir," Lily whimpered, her thighs spreading ever so slightly.

Night bobbed her head up, down, up, down. Her fingers *schlicked* into her sex again and again. She was growing more and more eager, her eyes closing when she slipped forward, then opening to look up at Buck when she slid her mouth back to the tip of his dick. The look in her eyes was still soft and submissive. Pat, meanwhile, had gotten his feet tangled in his pants. He managed to kick off his shoes and then his pants before staggering forward, cock bobbing in the open air. The only thing that shocked him was that he wasn't wilting at the sight of Buck's member.

Buck chuckled and pushed Night's head back and away from his member, which rested against her nose for a moment. Night breathed in, inhaling his scent like a drug addict. Her body quivered as she moaned, reaching up and cupping her breasts together. She was putting on a show for Buck, Pat realized. His cock ached as it grew even harder. Buck grinned down at her.

"You're addicted, huh?" he murmured.

"Oh yes..." Night purred.

"So, you don't mind if your boyfriend slips his tiny little pencil dick into someone else?" Buck asked.

"Can I keep sucking your cock?" Night asked, her voice desperate. "Please just... let me keep sucking that *amazing* cock."

Pat trembled, his hands grabbing onto Lily's hips. He couldn't stop himself. It wasn't even a dominant move, not really. He was holding her just to keep himself from collapsing to his knees, which quivered and shook as he heard Nightshade beg for more cock. Buck laughed, low and even.

"Well, since you said please," he said, casually. "I'll let you beg."

Night purred. Her soft, pink tongue darted out and she whispered hotly: "Please, let me fill my muzzle with your cock. I want to taste your cum. Fuck, I want to *live* on your cum. Let me suck you, let me be your little cock slut..." Her voice came in soft, eager pants and Buck laughed quietly. He looked at Pat, as if to say: *Look at what she does. Look at what she's become.* With his eyes still locked on Pat's, Buck's palm cupped the back of Night's head and pushed her forward. Her mouth opened wide and she sucked Buck right back into her mouth with a low, eager moan.

"Mmm," Buck growled, low in his throat. "Pencil dick. Put your pecker against my secretary."

Pat's cock pressed against the cleft of Lily's ass. The doe whimpered softly as Buck leaned forward. His hands grabbed onto Nightshade's ears like they were handlebars. His thumbs caressed her ear tips and Night trembled all over, her thighs spreading wide as she bucked her hips and her mouth in equal measures. She was now fingering herself with the wild abandon of a total whore.

Buck smirked. "Good. Now, Lily... you're thinking of me, huh?"

Lily nodded, desperately. "Yes! Fuck me Buck! Fuck me, please fuck me!"

"Well, bitch," Buck purred, addressing Pat. "Grind against her. Let her live out her fantasy."

Pat slipped his hips back, pressing the tip of his member against Lily's sex—following orders without a thought. She was radiating heat, and her dripping cunt soon made his member more than slick enough. As her juices dripped from his cock, he remained stiller than he had ever been in his entire life. Even his tail didn't move. He felt as if he was hanging between heart beats. For a brief moment, Pat wondered if she'd let him fuck her in the ass, since Nightshade never allowed it. But he pushed the thought from his mind. He wasn't in a position to decide anything, much less be opportunistic.

Buck purred. "Lily…"

The single word seemed to be enough for Lily to moan. "Please. Slide your big, fat dick into my tight, little pussy. Please, Buck, make me your *bitch*."

Pat still hesitated. He couldn't move. Not until Buck inclined his head—ever so slightly. Even with a girl writhing and begging for him, even with her juices literally slipping along his dick and dripping from his balls, Pat needed to see that tiny nod; that tiny indication that Buck wanted him to do it. That he, the pathetic little cuck in the room, could actually do something. With that nod, Pat pushed himself forward and felt his cock slide all the way into Lily's velvety opening. It felt delicious, and strange. He hadn't been in another girl in ages. He would have thought, before hilting himself in Lily, that being balls deep in a girl other than Nightshade would be…

Masculine. Powerful.

Look at me, he'd have said. *I'm Patrick, and I'm a player!*

That wasn't what it was like at all.

He began to fuck her forcefully, as if trying to impress her with sheer strength. As his balls slammed the doe's hard, little clit, her mouth opened and she moaned, her voice as sweet as music. "Ohhh *Buuuuuuck!*"

Pat's balls clenched and he nearly came from the intoxicating wrongness of it. That was the nightmare of nearly every red-blooded man that he knew. But he embraced this nightmare, and he grew to love it as he drew his cock back and slammed into Lily again. She was tighter than Nightshade, but she was clearly enjoying the hard, rough fucking as she began to buck her hips against his. Nightshade, meanwhile, was being dragged off Buck's cock by the ears, her mouth hanging open, her tongue lolling out. She panted like a bitch in heat, her eyes unfocused and hooded as she whimpered up at Buck.

"You want my cock in you, don't you bitch?" Buck purred.

"*Fuck* me, Buck!" Lily gasped, her fingernails digging into the varnished wood of the desk. "Fuck me! Fuck my slutty brains out!"

"Yessss," Night breathed. "Make me yours, Buck..."

Buck grinned. "Not yet... now's not the time." He instead surged to his feet. Night whimpered, and then she gasped as Buck gripped his cock with his hands. He started to pump his thick, massive member with slow, steady strokes. Night planted her hands on the ground, arching her back so that her chest thrust outward. Her amazing, plump breasts jiggled as she opened her mouth wide. Her entire posture said, as clear as day: *Do anything you want to me. Use me.*

Buck laughed. "Good bitch. Good little, slutty bitch. You need this, don't you?" His hand pumped and a single spurt of pre escaped from his cock. Night managed to catch it in her mouth as if it were choreographed. Pat watched the scene unfolding with wide eyes, his balls continuing to slap against Lily's clit with the familiar and intoxicating *pap pap pap* sound he had long associated with Nightshade when she was wild.

"Yes," Night whispered.

"What do you need, huh?" Buck asked, his voice tight.

"Your cum. Please, cum on me," Night moaned, softly.

"It's better than Pat's, isn't it?"

"Yesssss," Night hissed.

"You don't need his cum, do you?" Buck gasped out. He was barely holding back.

Pat felt himself driving faster and faster towards his own climax. Lily had already stopped moaning coherently. Instead, she was merely bucking back against him, her hips matching his tempo. Her eyes were closed and she had turned her head, pressing her muzzle and cheek against the desk. Her body trembled as she came again and again, her cunt tightening around Pat's dick. Pat, though, was too good a cuck to cum. His body had been trained, and in that moment, his mind was yoked utterly to Buck as the muscular cervine jerked his dick at Nightshade.

Buck hadn't let him cum.

"No, no," Night spoke, her voice coming out in a tumbling gasp. "Every time I drink cum, anyone's cum, I'll be thinking of yours. Pleeease, just... *paint* me."

"*Buck!*" Lily shuddered and came from the latest in a string of climaxes, harder than the previous, as if she had hit a new level of pure pleasure.

Her sex clenched on Pat's dick and Pat watched as Buck groaned quietly and loosed himself. Thick strands of hot, white cum splashed against Nightshade's breasts, soaking her fur. Some splashed her muzzle, but she caught it expertly, her tongue darting out to lick it all up. Nightshade was usually too proud to do facials, but she seemed to be content with the seed that painted along the side of her muzzle, dripping down to her breasts. More splashed her belly, her shoulders, and some even dribbled down her rapidly shifting forearm. Night, whose hand was still between her legs, moaned and came as well.

She panted softly as Buck remained poised over her. He grinned, and rather than falling limp, as anyone would in that situation, he remained standing. Erect and proud. He looked at Pat, smirking slightly.

"She's mine," he purred. "You can cum, if you think Lily will even notice."

Pat lost all control. He slammed into Lily like a wild animal, feeling himself utterly given over to Buck. It was like being possessed, and Lily did not help that feeling. Every thrust brought a new moan for Buck. Pat's hands went from her hips to her shoulders and he pinned her to the desk, the fierceness of their fucking knocking the screen down onto the keyboard with a clatter all four of them ignored.

It was enough to send Pat over an edge he had been clinging onto by the tips of his fingers. And the fall was as dark and deep and amazing as few others in his life. His balls surged and the same amount of spunk that had once taken twenty minutes of cleaning to get out of his keyboard splashed directly into Lily. Into another woman.

She shuddered from ears to hooves. Her tail twitched wildly against Pat's belly as his cum filled her.

Quiet descended on the office, with only the faint *click* of the settling room. Buck slowly sat down in his chair, sighing as Nightshade started to lick the cum from her body, whining softly.

Then a loud call-incoming sound filled the office. Ezra—and it was Ezra right now, not Buck—sat up, slapping his half-hard dick against a very surprised Nightshade's face. She yelped and jerked away as Ezra grabbed the screen, trying to right the monitor from where it had been knocked over.

"Bugger!" he said. "It's Mr. Moench!"

"What?" Pat managed to say that one word. It was weird how hard it was to articulate even that. But Ezra was busy helping Night to her feet.

She stood, her knees shaking visibly. Ezra rubbed her shoulder with a smile while he whispered something into her ear. She giggled softly, slapping at his chest—and a feeling that was most unwelcome and unsettling came over Pat. That wasn't Buck. That was Ezra being playful with his girlfriend. It was one thing for Buck to 'claim' Nightshade.

It...

It was another when-

"Out! Now! It's Mr. Moench from NASA!" Ezra said, pointing to the door, his voice startling Pat from his reverie.

Pat, Lily and Nightshade managed to get out before the door was shut right in their faces in the blink of an eye. Pat opened his mouth, then looked down. His pants, shirt and shoes were still in the room, but safely out of view of the webcam. He could hear the sound of Ezra's voice—light, cheery, and only slightly out of breath.

"Douuug, how's it hanging? Still growing that mustache I see? So, I need to ask you about the Hohmann Transfers your team worked out for the Titan mission..."

Pat looked at Lily. Somehow, she had managed to get her clothes in her hands before she had been booted out of the room. She grinned at him, shyly. "S-So, uh, my number is-"

"Not needed, lassie," Nadia said, the Scottish tones of her upbringing filtering out more than usual. Her voice was light, cheerful and lethal all at the same time. Her hands cradled Pat's chest, her nails pressing lightly to his fur. She circled one of his nipples.

"Oh, uh, well-" Lily stammered. "Thanks for, uh... the sex?" She sounded like she wasn't quite sure if that was the right way to thank Pat, but he smiled back shyly.

"I taught him *all* of that," Nadia said, her grin definitely malevolent. "Now, why don't you toddle off and get Patty-Cakes here a bathrobe or something?"

Lily paled, then turned and ran down the stairs, not even bothering to get dressed.

Pat felt extremely exposed. He coughed. "S-So, uh..." he looked back at Nadia. "Feeling possessive?"

"I don't have to," Nadia said, smirking slightly. She kissed Pat's cheek.

Pat tried to be comforted by that. But part of him—a growing part, dark and deep like the waters of the ocean—wasn't so sure how she meant it. She didn't have to be worried because she was confident in his affections? Or was it because she didn't need only his anymore?

CHAPTER 7

"Getting home was its own adventure, but let's just say that Londoners are jaded folk. They've seen odder things than a giraffe in a bathrobe. I didn't even think to ask for my clothes back. I was pretty sure Buck wouldn't have let me have them anyway."

* * *

Pat laid back into the sofa with Nadia sprawled across his chest in the least dignified way imaginable. Her head lolled to the side, her thigh pressed to his crotch, her breasts to his chest. She let one arm dangle whiled another was propped up near Pat's head, her finger tracing a slow, steady line around one of his ears. Pat felt completely and utterly drained. He could barely summon the strength to move his hand to pat the back of Nadia's head.

"That was nice," he mumbled.

"Mmhmm," Nadia said, her voice soft.

"I can't believe…" Pat said, letting his head rest back against the armrest of the sofa. "That you sucked Ezra, er, Buck off for, um, what?" He paused, thinking of the time he spent working, trying to match it up against Nadia's shifts at the Safari, and when she'd had to have arrived at Ezra's office, then combined the amount of time that he had spent waiting before calling them. "Two hours?"

Nadia giggled. "Pat, I'm good. But I'm not a *goddess*-"

"Who is spreading these filthy lies?" Pat asked, faux-outraged, managing to actually sit up for a few seconds before he lounged back against the sofa again.

Nadia nipped at his belly with her teeth. Once he had settled, she continued. "I'm not *magical*. There." She grinned and Pat made a hand-waving gesture, as if he wasn't entirely sure if that was the case. Nadia stuck her tongue out at him. "I can't suck anyone off for two hours, because I *didn't* suck him off for two hours. Those two hours were spent with him teasing me, finger fucking me, talking dirty, showing off his status and his muscles…" She sighed. "I could nuzzle his tummy for *hours*."

Pat blinked. "H-Hours, huh?"

"Pat, you dork," Nadia said, her voice rich with amusement. "I saw *you* drooling over his physique. I believe *I* am allowed a bit of a nuzzle now and then." Her eyes glittered.

Pat felt a flush covering his face from the tops of his ossicones to the tip of his muzzle. He coughed and stammered. "A-Admired is not exactly the right word, I think." He was trying to sound confident and breezy. Instead, he was pretty sure that a lot of his fear slipped into his words. That fear triggered the 'hunt, stalk, pounce' instinct in Nadia. He could see it, glinting in her emerald eyes.

"Patty-Cakes, Patty-Cakes, Patty-Cakes," Nadia purred, airily. "Everything about Buck intimidates you. That's what I *like* about it." She grinned. "About him. About you. My sweet little giraffe." She stuck her nose against the base of the bathrobe he got from Lily, pushing it aside ever so slightly, revealing his own belly muscles. Her nose pressed against him and she sighed and breathed in. Her nose rubbed slowly against him, tracing out the lines of his abdominal muscles with the tip of her soft, wet nose. Her eyes closed and she crooned, quietly. "Maybe not so *little*." She started to lick him gently, as if cleaning away the sweat of the many, many, many gym sessions that had built this body. Pat grinned down at her, his finger reaching down to rub the join of ear and skull. Nadia shivered with pleasure, her ears twitching as she writhed against him. "Mmmmmhhh!"

But Pat wondered…

If she liked him being intimidated by Buck, should he lean into it? But if he did, would that intimidation become real? There was an element of truth to it. But if it'd make her happier…

He nodded slowly. "Not a patch on him, huh?" he murmured.

Nadia looked up at him. Her eyes narrowed and her grin became cruel. "No." She flicked his belly as she started to move up, her palms pressing to his thighs, using just an edge of her nails. Her voice crooned. "Buck could break you in half and that gets you *hard*, doesn't it?"

Pat blushed furiously. Okay. He was hard. Now. "N-No, I…" He trailed off at Night's—and it was Night right now—look.

Her ears flicked, and her mischievous grin widened. "So tell me instead… what was it like fucking another woman?"

Pat gulped. His exhausted body became suddenly rigid like steel, and a cold shiver began to spread through him. Night laughed. "It's not like I could ever *care* about who you fuck… not when *Buck* is around to give me the dick I need. The dick you never. Ever. *Ever* could." Her grin was wide. Her nipples thrust out against her thin top—everything about her screamed her lust. Pat's member ached against his jeans."

"W-Well, I…uh…I wasn't…" He squirmed, trying to relieve the tension against his cock. "Buck insisted."

"I know he did," Night said, her tone edging with a growl. "Is that all you can think about? What *Buck* told you to do, you little. Pathetic…" Her voice crooned as she leaned in close, whispering into his ear. "Bitch?"

Pat swallowed. What did he think? He hadn't expected to be fucking another woman when he agreed to all of this—and he had *never* expected Nadia to act like this. It was something fierce and intimidating, and it made him feel as if Buck was looming in the room. Grinding his massive cock against Nadia's back as she leaned forward and whispered sweet poison into his ear. It was addictive. It was horrifying. He loved it. His eyes half closed and he managed to squeak out: "Yes…"

"Mmm…" Night bit his ear gently, then pressed herself against him. Her arm looped around his belly, she hooked her thigh over his. It was as if there was no way that she could possibly mold herself against him more. Like every inch of her fur screamed to be pressed to him. "God, you're such a perfect cuck, Pat, I love it. God, I'm so wet and horny right now…" she laughed, her voice shaky. "Please. Take me to the bedroom and just fuck my brains out."

Pat felt the scene loosen. He laughed and then looked at her. "Buck gets you that wet?"

"*You* do," she murmured. And it was Nadia who molded herself against him now.

Pat grinned, then grabbed her. He swung her into his arms, and Nadia only slightly struggled. It was a paradox: She wanted to cling to him, but she also wanted to be held in his arms. She wanted to be swung around like a damsel in a daring story, but she also didn't want to give up contact of fur on fur, skin on skin. But her lusts decided the moment and she sprawled in his arms with the languid, fluid grace of a dancer, her arms looped around his neck. Pat turned and hurried, having to go sidelong through the corridor to the bedroom.

The absolute last thing in the world he needed right now was to bonk Nadia's head into the wall while carrying her to the boudoir.

Once there, he dropped Nadia onto the bed. His hands grabbed onto the bathrobe belt, and he swore that in the time it took to untie it, Nadia had gone from her modest, around-the-house clothing to buck naked. Her full, pendulous breasts sagged ever so slightly to either side as she arched her back and kicked her panties off her ankle with a dainty little flick. Her pussy proved, more than her eyes, more than her panting, more than the wanton way she spread her thighs, just how badly she wanted him at that moment. It was soaked. The black folds of her cunny were dripping with her arousal and she panted heavily as Pat stood there, gaping.

Nadia laughed—a hitched, ragged laugh. "*Patrick.*"

"Right!" Pat shook himself, then pulled at the mostly-untied belt. The rasp of fabric unwrapping was unnaturally loud in the room—cutting over the pant, the whimper, the slick sound of Nadia's fingers spreading her pussy. The bathrobe parted and Pat felt his cock springing into the air. Nadia's back arched ever so slightly more, and if there was a more inviting scene than her pose at the moment—spread, wanting, dripping—Pat couldn't have imagined it. He dropped the robe to the floor and crawled onto the bed with Nadia, and before he knew it, his mouth and hers met. Her tongue swept into his mouth and her hips locked around his. Her ankles hooked, one over the other, as she practically dragged him into her.

Pat grunted, low and hot. His body shuddered and his hands slipped under Nadia's back, dragging her against him as he rocked her almost off the bed—slamming into her again and again and again. It was a fierce, hot, tight fuck—not merely because her sex clenched on him like a silken glove—it was also because her legs refused to let him move more than an inch away with every slamming thrust. His hips and hers slapped together and his balls pounded against her ass like a drum.

Nadia broke the kiss, only to immediately bite down on his shoulder, shuddering as she moaned into his body. Pat barely noticed the faint pain that flared around her mouth; he was too focused on nailing her to the bed. His hands gripped her back and she threw her head back, wailing in pure bliss.

"Yes! God yes! Fuck me! Yes!" She cried out—loud enough to drive Pat over the edge. His whole body locked up, his back tightening, his head tossing backwards as he groaned, long and low and eager. His balls clenched and his fingers dug into her fur as he moaned a single name.

"Nadia!" He gasped for air—desperate. His heart hammered as he felt his seed springing from his cock, slicking his balls. Nadia twitched under him, her hips spread, her back arched and her breasts rising and falling with the movement of her chest. She breathed in the same ragged, desperate way that he was—her eyes unfocused and her jaw hanging open.

"God... *damn*," she whispered as Pat slowly slid himself down to his elbows. His body ached as if he had been running for miles, not merely fucking for a few minutes. His shoulders quivered and he had to work to keep from simply squashing Nadia under his weight. Nadia herself seemed as interested in unlocking her legs from around his hips as she was in eating a salad.

"Yeah," Pat whispered.

Nadia grinned at him, shakily. She leaned in and kissed him—and there didn't need to be more words after that. Pat slowly softened and just as slowly slid from her. But all the way, they didn't stop touching. Pat drew Nadia in close, and her arms nestled against her chest as her eyes closed. Looking over his shoulder, he could see her right arm tossed out onto the bed, carelessly. And there, glinting in a shaft of moonlight through the blinds, was the ring that Buck had given her.

Pat hadn't realized how fragile his sense of well-being had been until he felt it quiver on seeing that ring. He clung to Nadia just a bit closer.

"*Almost* as good as Buck," Nadia murmured, her eyes closed. From the little, playful smile on her lips, Pat had a sinking feeling that she thought that would rev him up even more.

It did the exact fucking opposite.

* * *

"*That melange of insecurity, happiness and fear was intoxicating. But my inner demons hadn't gone silent. If I had thought I had felt the worst of them, though, that was only because we hadn't reached the gym yet. Oh... the gym.*"

* * *

Pat was on the treadmill, a week and a half after the office. That was how he would always think about it—as the office. Every other office would be compared to that sex-scented, hazy, dreamlike time inside of Ezra's keep. Buck filling Night's throat, Lily's sex tight around his own dick, Buck's voice wrung from her throat. And then the aftermath. Nadia driving him to the edge of madness with lust and humiliation before fucking him and ending it by murmuring in his ear about Buck. Twice, he had felt a worry about how far it was going, how he considered stopping it. But twice, he had seen how happy Nadia had been—and knew he never ever *ever* could.

Pat forced his brain away from Nadia, as he was wearing tight shorts for working out. The last thing he wanted to do was try jogging on the treadmill with a stiffy, especially since there was a rather large and intimidating rhino on the machine next to him.

The rhino was running about half as fast as him and was a curious mixture of age, muscle and fat. He also had stuck earbuds into his tiny ears and turned on what sounded like classical music from the few strains of strings and trumpets that reached Pat. Since he wasn't interested in talking—and thus distracting Pat from his imagination—Pat looked around the rest of the gym. A few of the other treadmills to his left were unused. But then, at the edge of the room, was a lioness whose ass and tail were having exactly the wrong impact on Pat's brain if he wanted to cool down. Pat swung his head back, thinking maybe he could at least talk to the rhino. But he was already off, heading back to the locker room.

And so, he looked straight forward, clenched his jaw, and tried to watch the people walking by the front windows at the far end of the Muscle Bros. Heavy Lifting Gym for Cool Guys, as Pat jokingly referred to it.

It was open to all comers and was cheaper than the 24-hour gym that was slightly closer to the flat. Since he was coming to the gym to maintain his physique, Pat didn't mind the extra walk. Nadia herself loved the gym, mostly because she loved showing up men who thought they could hit on her. Pat looked over and saw that a husky who clearly skipped leg days was flexing in a none-too-subtle way before her as he lifted up a pair of dumbbells.

Nadia was on an incline bench press, spreading herself wide, her breasts filling her workout clothes in the most fetching way imaginable. She simply smirked at the husky. Pat grinned—then started as a familiar, burly-looking deer walked up behind the husky and slid an arm around his shoulder. The husky froze, then stepped away, practically running as Nadia looked at Buck with clear admiration.

And that was the moment.

The moment where Pat's screaming voice—that tiny, whispering voice that his lust and kink had gagged and bound and tossed down a flight of stairs from the moment they decided on a safeword—came back. And it came back with a vengeance, bursting up the flight of stairs that was his spine and grabbing his ossicones, yanking them hard and shrieking.

That should be you!

And Pat realized it was right.

But before Pat could get his head back on straight, Buck had already moved behind Nadia to seemingly spot her. The two talked and laughed. Was it Buck? Maybe it was Ezra? It was hard to tell at a distance without hearing his tone of voice. And that confusion only made the screaming voice get louder and more insistent. Buck was a character. Ezra was the man. The bigger, richer, smarter man. The man planning to colonize the solar system. The man who could buy Nadia a gold ring with his pocket change. The man she thought of every time Pat fucked her.

The man whose name she moaned in bed when he thrust into her.

Pat slapped down on the cancel track button and the treadmill started to slow. He puffed and panted and hopped off, then walked over.

"So, I thought I had carried it off fine, when suddenly, Doug says: Ezzy, where's your trousers?" Ezra was saying jovially as Pat walked over.

"Hey," Pat said, his voice low.

The two of them looked up at him. Nadia looked quizzical, flicking her ears in an almost questioning way. Ezra looked faintly uncertain—but then Pat pointed at him.

"She's *my* girlfriend," he said, his voice tight.

The screaming voice was mumbling something. Pat couldn't hear it over the thundering sound of his own heart, the quickness of his breath. It wasn't all from running, not even close. Ezra cocked his head. And slowly, like Dr. Jekyll becoming Mr. Hyde, Buck settled onto Ezra's features. His hands went to Nadia's shoulders, and he smirked.

"I don't know," he said. "I seem to be doing all the boyfriend work. You even fuck her this past week?"

Pat had. He knew he had. He opened his mouth to say he had, but Buck cut him off.

"With a real dick? Without her moaning *my* name?" Buck's voice was chocolate laced with razor blades. Pat squirmed and felt his cock hardening despite himself. The screaming voice tried to say something, but Buck was already helping Night—and she *was* Night at that moment—to her feet. He jerked his head. "Come on."

And like a meek little cuck, Pat followed.

The doors to the locker room opened to reveal two older gentlemen looking over at them. One of them was the rhino that Pat had been jogging beside. The other was an otter with gray in his fur and whiskers. The two were really polar opposites. The rhino big and chunky, the otter more lithe, but both wore their age on their sleeve, easily twenty years older than Buck. Despite that, Buck sent them a look that made the two of them shut up and go back to their conversation. Soon, the trio arrived in the shower stalls near the back of the room. Pat was set at the door, stopped and rooted in place by a single glance from Buck. As Pat stood there, Buck grinned and nodded.

"You can keep watch. It's all your bitch ass is good for."

Night shivered excitedly, her ears alert. Buck grabbed the hem of her shirt and tugged it up over her head. She moaned as her shirt hit the ground and Buck's hands grasped her sports bra before discarding it as easily as her top. Her ample breasts briefly swayed in the free air before Buck's hands cupped them. His fingers were merciless, pinching, tweaking and twisting. Night only hissed softly; she didn't mind the hurt, it seemed. Her knees quivered and she let loose with a low keen.

Buck grinned. "Get her knickers in her mouth, bitch," he said.

Pat stepped forward. He knelt behind Nightshade and removed her shoes and socks, setting them aside. He shakily reached up and tugged her tight workout pants down. Her delicious, heart shaped rear jiggled as he took a hold of her functional, simple panties and pulled them down. Her feet lifted off the ground and set back down with soft clicks of toenails on tiles. She gasped again as Buck leaned forward and took a dark nipple in his mouth. He sucked, slurped, then drew back with a smack of his chops. Night opened her mouth to moan loudly. She couldn't help herself.

Meek and gentle, Pat balled up her panties and set them in her mouth. She gurgled happily, softly, her mouth closing tightly around the fabric. Buck then pushed Pat backwards, hard enough that he almost fell on his spotted ass. He stood in the doorway, his cock aching, his heart hammering. He looked over his shoulder once, twice, three times. Each time, he didn't see anyone coming. Each time, he looked back and saw the love of his life moving closer and closer to fucking around on him again.

But this time, he didn't want it. And Night had no idea. His throat tightened and he knew what he had to do.

He…

Oh…

His eyes softened as he watched that massive cock slap between her ass cheeks. Buck smirked and then ground the tip of his cock against Night's asshole. Night had never done anal with Pat, ever, despite his frequent requests. She had always said she didn't enjoy it.

Pat's heart froze as Night whimpered happily, pushing and grinding her rump against Buck's cock head. Was she signalling she was open to anal? It was always off limits before. A sickening mixture of jealousy and curiosity spasmed through Pat as he watched. But Buck clicked his tongue and whispered quietly. "Nah... didn't bring lube." Night's mouth swung open and her panties fell partially out of her mouth, her moan growing slightly louder. She actually seemed to be a few moments away from offering her ass, offering that ass she refused to let Pat fuck... to Buck.

Pat was so thrown by that, he barely noticed the footsteps behind him until it was too late.

"What the-"

The voice was deep and rich and made Pat freeze. His head snapped around and he saw that the rhino and the otter had arrived. The two of them gasped, their eyes wide as saucers, their mouths hanging open. The rhino's horn bobbed forward as he blinked slowly, his mouth closing again, then opening.

"What the devil is going on here?"

"Why, a very good time, sir," Buck said, his voice arrogance incarnate. He flicked his bushy tail and jerked his head. His fingers darted forward, tugging the panties from Night's mouth, now that the gag was no longer needed. Or wanted. "Why don't you two join us. We could use some real cocks. Our giraffe here isn't packing enough for his lady."

The two older men looked at Pat, dumbfounded. Pat saw the look in their eyes; initial shock slowly turning into comprehension. The rhino was steadily growing more and more eager, his eyes glinting. The otter remained confused for a few moments longer. Then a light flicked on across his entire expression and he reminded Pat that otters were predators. Hunters. The otter stepped up behind Pat, slapping his back with a sharp-toothed grin.

"Bringing a pop gun to an artillery duel, huh?" he asked.

The rhino stepped forward and put his hands on his shirt, tugging it up and off. As he stripped, Buck did the same and maneuvered Night to the linoleum floor with him. The large deer sat down, spreading his legs, and took Night by the wrist—his fingers briefly touching the gold ring adorning her hand—and motioned for her to straddle him. She did so without pause, sitting with her ass to him, allowing his rigid cock to tower before her belly. It reached her pierced navel.

Buck instructed Night to guide him, and she eagerly caressed his throbbing member and arched herself to slip his cocktip against her pussy. She whined, her voice growing louder. It occurred to Pat that despite everything that had happened since Buck entered their lives, he had yet to see him actually fuck Nightshade. The sick thrill of seeing the act pulled at him, and yet, he felt something was distracting him.

Pat looked from Night to Buck, and found the deer was looking square into his eyes. Pat shriveled under that dominant look. Then he felt movement to his side, and looked to see that the two older men were naked now, while Pat was still squirming in his gym clothes.

Curiosity drove him to observe their nakedness. The otter had a pot belly and a noticeable tuft of chest fur. His cock wasn't as thick as Pat's, but was long and curved. The rhino's cock was about an inch or two shorter than Buck's, but made up for it with immense thickness. His gray shaft filled his hand, his wrist nestling against the curve of his broad belly. He had enough muscle to make him more of a bruiser than a blubberer, but there was still plenty of fat; the fat of someone who enjoyed their life a great deal. And now, he was rubbing the tip of his thick cock against Night's nose.

Night made a quiet, curious *hmm* sound. But Buck squeezed her shoulders encouragingly. The squeeze made her perk up and her ears flattened back against her head as she breathed, her whole body shuddering as she drew in the rhino's musk.

"You're an eager little minx, aren't you?" the rhino murmured.

"She's a total slut for real men," Buck purred. "This little wimp can't even get her to beg."

Night's hand gripped the rhino's cock and squeezed. He sighed, and the otter moved around to Night's other side. Night rocked against Buck's cock—Buck taking his time, slipping his tip in and out, adding a delicious counterpoint to the movement of Night's hips. Buck caught Pat's eyes again. Pat didn't break eye contact, even though he desperately wanted to watch, to see. And then Pat's will snapped and he looked down at the spreading folds of Night's cunt as Buck stopped teasing and began sliding home. He made it halfway before Night shuddered and squirmed. He ran his hands comfortingly along her hips, and Night breathed and dropped her weight, taking more of his length.

Gravity did the trick and the last of Buck's member slipped into her. His balls nestled themselves against Night's clit. He was completely inside her. That monstrously large cock was nestled snugly in her to the hilt. It seemed impossible, but she somehow managed it, and this was only the second time she'd had taken him vaginally. That Pat knew of.

Pat felt his mind fracture at the thought that Night was permanently ruined by Buck, unable to enjoy anything less than his monster member that she had adjusted her body to accept. As if to confirm, Night's thighs trembled in a deep orgasm, her hands closing tightly around the two older men's cocks. She groaned low, desperately, her tail lifting upwards. The otter hissed, ducking his head forward.

"See that?" Buck whispered.

Pat nodded.

"What's that?" Buck purred, sliding his cock nearly all the way out of her.

The screaming voice was trying to say something. It felt like it was coming through a thick cloth wrapped around Pat's head. He could barely hear his own voice as he whispered.

"A... a real man..."

"*Her* real man," Buck said, sliding himself all the way inside Night again. As he spoke, Night began rocking her hips forward. The rhino reached down to squeeze one shoulder, keeping her rooted in place. Her breasts jiggled as the otter breathed in slow, quick gasps. Her palms slicked up and down their dicks, both of them aimed at her face, her chest. Night's face was slack with pleasure and decadent delight. Her eyes were half closed and hazy. "She's *mine* now. She'll do anything I want. Even jerk off strangers in a fucking shower. Huh, dear? Isn't that right?"

Buck slightly spread his legs, giving Pat a better view, and then started to thrust into Nightshade. Every thrust made Pat want to run forward, to grab him, to stop him But he was right. Night shuddered in orgasmic bliss after his cock had plunged home just two times. Her hands, though, didn't squeeze any tighter. Even now, she worked the two cocks like a pro.

This wasn't her first time in this kind of situation. Memories of late night conversations plagued Pat at that moment. Stories of Night's wild twenties. Of her dominatrix days as a queen, of wild parties, being worshipped and catered to by countless men. Of indulging in her every desire, exploring every kink and deviance. Of sucking and fucking strangers. Buck was dragging her back to that, and...

And she looked like she loved it.

As Pat watched, her head turned and she sucked the rhino's cock tip into her muzzle, her tongue drawing slow circles around his lengthy foreskin before taking him into her. As her head bobbed, Buck started to pick up speed. He moved faster and faster, his hips driving into her like a steam locomotive. His balls slapped against her pussy loud enough to almost ride roughshod over the rhino's low, eager moan. Night's breasts transcribed perfect circles, some of Buck's spittle still dripping from the nipple he had slathered attention on earlier.

Spittle, too, dripped from the cock she was sucking. She released it, then turned and took the otter into her mouth. The otter leaned his head back and hissed eagerly. "F-Fuck, you blow me better than my students," he laughed roughly, his paw caressing the back of Night's head. Night slurped her muzzle back, grinning slyly at him.

Pat winced. These men were old; way past their prime. These were the kind of men Night would often complain about when she would come home from work. With her beauty and presence, she could have any man she wanted. She had standards. But now she was so hungry for cock she would take any presented before her. Pat looked pitifully on as Night switched between the cocks, trails of drool and pre connecting them to her like spiderwebs. If only these men knew who she was; how lucky they were to have her service them like this.

Suddenly, Night's eyes widened and she shuddered, her hands tightening enough to cause both of the older men to hiss. Pat, his belly roiling with nerves and horror and excitement, saw why.

Buck had reached forward and planted his palm right on her deliciously firm belly. His middle finger—long and broad and oh so skilled—had landed right on her clit and was slowly circling it, using just enough pressure to set off fireworks behind Night's eyes. Her hands started to work faster and faster as she hung her head forward and shuddered around the cock filling her. Buck thrust roughly, clearly not trying to control himself. This was in public so it had to be quick. Even though it was nowhere near the length of the time in the office, it still dragged on like a hideous scene in a torture dungeon for Pat. Still, he was fairly certain he'd never been this close to cumming without touching himself before. Because, screaming voice or no…

Night was still beautiful.

Buck's thrusts rapidly arched into a climax. He shuddered and came hard as he thrust into her one last time, burying himself deep inside her. His head ducked forward and his antlers clacked against the wall. Pat could see Bucks's balls twitch with every blast of cum.

"Fuck yes, fill me up," Night growled, her head tilted forward, her bangs covering her eyes. Her body convulsed in tiny tremors as she basked in orgasmic bliss while her pussy was filled to the brim by Buck for the second time. She absentmindedly jerked the cocks on either side of her, and then took the otter back into her mouth, sucking him urgently.

"Shit, this is too much," the otter said, his back arching. Night smirked and drew her head back, luridly showing off the long, glistening shaft while still keeping the cock head nestled between her lips. Then, suddenly she pushed forward and took the whole length into her muzzle again, her throat noticeably bulging.

The otter took her by the ears and thrust into her quickly, his hairy belly pushing against her nose, making her suck in air out of the corners of her mouth. His mustache bristled and he barred his sharp teeth as his climax approached.

"Oh fuck yes, take it love," he groaned as he urgently pumped his cock down Night's throat. Then she deftly put her fingers around the base of his cock and pushed him back so that his cock exited her.

A moment passed, a moment that felt like an eternity, and then a jet of cum released from his cock and splashed across Night's face, followed by thick strands of cum that splattered onto her full breasts; white against dark fur. She closed her eyes and moaned happily as more strings of thick cum spurted over her body from the otter's wildly bucking cock. Some splashed her shoulders, others dripped as low as her belly. It left her glistening. Her eyes were closed, her face split with a wide, beatific grin.

The rhino had been grinding into her free hand the whole time, and she began stroking him in earnest. She tried to take him in her mouth again, strings of cum dripping down onto his member only to be pushed back into her mouth. The rhino grunted, and carefully held her head in his enormous hands as he tried to push more of his massive girth into her, but it resulted in little progress. Only a bit less than a third of him could fit into her muzzle, and the frustration he felt at that was growing more pronounced.

"Damn it, I can't get in there," he muttered. He pulled back, eliciting a sound from Night's mouth akin to a cork being pulled from a bottle. The look on Night's face changed from lurid to disappointed. She looked at

Pat, as if to say she were sorry the entertainment wasn't going as planned.

"I'm trying my best. You're just *really* thick," Night said, her voice almost a whine. She glanced between Pat and the rhino, mild panic hiding in her eyes.

"Your jaw must still be tired after the office visit," Buck mused from behind her. He had been growing softer inside her, and a steady dribble of cum had been collecting around his balls. With a slow, explosive sigh, Buck pulled out of her cunt, letting more of his cum pour out of her and onto the ground.

Buck smirked at Pat, then slid his arm around Nightshade as she panted. He drew her into his embrace, leaning forward and kissing her over her shoulder. She tilted her head to kiss him lovingly back. If he cared she had just been sucking off other men, he didn't show it. Their tongues played together as Pat squirmed and writhed inside, absentmindedly stroking himself through his gym shorts. Night broke the kiss, gasping and panting something faintly incoherent, her eyes out of focus.

Buck made a surprised face and then a wicked smile crossed his lips. He looked at Pat and whispered to Night some more, before giving her a quick kiss—all the while never breaking eye contact with the giraffe. Night turned to face Pat, her eyes looking from him to the floor, as her face seemed to morph between guilt and excitement.

"Well, my rhinoceros friend, we can't have you leave without getting off," Buck said, still not breaking eye contact with Pat. A shiver ran through Pat's body and his stomach twisted into a knot as he wondered what the cervine had in store.

One of his dark hands found its way to Night's breast and began to lovingly roll and squeeze it in his powerful palm. The other trailed down to her groin and began to tease her clit, making her squirm and softly pant. "Perhaps her cunt would be a better option. After all, I've already stretched and lubricated it. If… her boyfriend is okay with it, that is," Buck said, his voice like dark chocolate.

The rhino chuckled and turned to look at Pat, who despite being taller than him, now felt like the smallest person in the room.

"I'd never turn down good pussy," the rhino said. "What say you? You're her… man, aren't you?"

Pat tried to lick his lips. Suddenly everyone in the room was staring at him, awaiting his response. The room felt incredibly wide and empty, the only sounds being the echo of a dripping faucet somewhere, and Night's soft panting as Buck teased her while waiting for Pat's response.

It occurred to Pat that at this moment, all the power was in his hands. After all, as Night had once told him before, the submissive is the real one in control. They have the power to end everything with a word. A safe-word. He could use it, and end all of this.

But the whole situation was for his sake as well. At the start of this, he had told them there were no limits, after all. Night had warned him he was overdoing it. but he had also told her he trusted her.

Trust.

He trusted her to keep his feelings in mind during these sessions. Despite her indulgences, surely she was keeping an eye on him?

The rhino shifted impatiently, and Pat blinked as he was brought back from deep thought. This guy was a stranger. There would be no attachments. Pat didn't even know his name. Despite his caution, a part of him was incredibly turned on by the prospect of a complete stranger getting a taste of Night, as if Buck fucking her wasn't enough.

He looked at Night, who gazed back at him with half-lidded eyes. Despite what she would tell him about supporting his decision, he knew from her expression she was eager to have that cock inside her.

And… deep down, he was eager for her to as well.

Pat summoned his pride and straightened his shoulders. His own cock, which had softened to half mast, began to throb back to full hardness, straining against his shorts as he cleared his throat and made his decision.

"She's all yours."

CHAPTER 8

"Yeah, I am a bit of an idiot. But saying the exact wrong thing did have one upside: What followed was, by far, the hottest thing that had happened in my life thus far."

* * *

"Are you sure, Patty-Cakes?" Night—or was it Nadia—asked, biting her lip.

"Yes," Pat said, without thinking. His head was spinning so fast that he wasn't sure, right now, if it was a lie or not. He wanted Nadia to be happy. But his member ached against his palms. He shook his head, then laughed, saying: "A-After all, I still haven't cum yet."

Buck laughed. "I think you're developing a tolerance. It's going to take more and more men fucking her to get you off, hm?" He gave Night's neck a lick. "Maybe we'll have to throw a party and have dozens of men take turns with her," he purred. Night, her knees quivering, moaned at the suggestion. Buck grinned and gave her pussy lips a slap.

"You like that idea, huh?" he murmured, softly. Night nodded mutely, then gasped as Buck caught her up from behind. His large fingers cupped her breasts, tweaked her nipples. He drew her in close and grinned over her shoulder at Pat. Night squirmed, whimpering softly, as Buck once again reached between her thighs. He started to fingerfuck her then—his digits plunging into her sex. Crooking. Rubbing. Night gasped, her eyes going hooded, her jaw hanging open as she wallowed at Buck's touch.

"Just getting her prepped," the deer crooned.

Pat gulped—and watched in awe as, in a shockingly short time, Night came. Her juices slipped along Buck's wrist as her knees went out. Buck let her slither out of his hands and to the floor, where she planted her elegant hands on either side of the shower's drain. She panted heavily, her head ducked forward. "Nice and ready for every man in this gym to take a round, huh?" Buck crooned.

Pat's eyes bulged at even the suggestion of that, but before he could think or speak or even breathe, Buck snapped his fingers and jerked his head at Pat. the giraffe moved without thinking, stepping forward as Buck lifted up Night's arms encouragingly. "Help your lady up," he said, and Pat did so, helping his lovely mistress to her feet. She pressed against him, the otter's cum on her breasts soaking into Pat's shirt. Normally that would bother him, but he didn't care. At this moment, all that mattered was that she was in his arms.

"I love you," Nadia whispered into the crook of his neck.

The words, simple and reassuring, made Pat's heart soar. He wanted to respond, but all he could do was hold her tighter. Nadia leaned in to give him a kiss on the cheek, before taking a step back and breaking the embrace. Pat looked her up and down. She was so glorious—her curvaceous body shone with a freshly cleaned edge. The cum that splattered her body, that dripped from her snout and smeared through her fur, glistened as if a heavenly light shone on it. None of it compared to the slickness glittering between her thighs, trailing down like shimmering spiderwebs. Night was clearly ready for the next round, even after being fucked from two ends like a plaything. She embodied a predatory edge that was unquestionable.

And again, Pat felt the creeping feeling of ineptitude crawl up his spine. Why would such a magnificent creature put up with him? He was just a lowly journalist. He had no money. No prestige. He didn't even have a cock as big as…

Buck casually walked out of the shower and motioned with his hand.

Pat's ears perked up as he heard the heavy sounds of the bulky rhino stomping past him. Nightshade grinned at Pat. She was going to rub this in his nose and not hold back in front of total strangers. His member ached in his pants and he started to mutely slide his palm up and down his cock, feeling the fabric rub against it. Slowly. Carefully. He didn't want to rush— the idea of being seen as premature filled him with so much shame that he nearly started to rush just to get mocked for it. Night chuckled at the sight of him touching himself—then turned to acknowledge the bulk of the rhino, who now filled the shower door.

Part of Pat groaned. He knew that if there was a time to use his safe-word, it was earlier, when her eyes had met his before the mask had come down and the scene had resumed.

When he had remained silent.

The rhino's gray hand was terribly visible against Nightshade's ebony fur. His palm casually cupped one of her large breasts, fondling her and drawing her close, making the jackal gasp in pleasure. The rhino began to gently tweak her nipple, twisting with just enough force to make Night's back arch and her legs spread. He leaned forward and took her muzzle in his lips, his kisses practically enveloping her snout. She reached down and stroked his enormous cock, her svelte fingers running only top to base, unable to encircle the whole thing. Night looked so very happy.

The rhino grinned. "This little bitch is ready for her round two... and I'm ready to get my shot." His hand reached down, gripping the base of his cock, taking it from her hand. Night instead put her arms around his wide shoulders.

"How do you want me?" she mused.

"Against the wall," the rhino said, nodding his head to the far end of the shower. They positioned themselves towards it, the rhino casually cupping an entire ass cheek in one of his hands.

Pat felt an arm slide around his shoulder, and he turned to see Buck smirking at him. It occurred to Pat he had never been this close to him before, and the raw masculinity of the deer nearly floored him. A strong scent of musk, sharp and dangerous like gun powder, hit his nostrils as Buck slowly stroked his incredible member, still dripping in spunk and Night's juices.

"You surprise me, Pat," Buck said calmly.

"O-oh?" Pat squeaked.

"Yeah. You're even more of a cuck than I imagined."

Pat scowled. Buck laughed and slapped him on the back. It was, for a brief moment, something he could imagine Ezra doing. But before he wondered if the deer had slipped character, he was practically guided over to the scene unfolding in the shower stall.

"You should be there to assist her," Buck said. "Give her assistance. She's going to need it, with a cock that big."

Pat gulped, and then looked over as the large gray shape of the rhino slowly ground against the smaller ebony body of Nightshade. She was bent over, her ass stuck out, her ears pinned back against her scalp with excitement as the rhino began to tease his cock against her oozing folds, slipping against her forcefully. She leaned against the shower wall, her palms and breasts pressed against the cold tiles.

"What are you waiting for?" Buck sneered. "Get over there already."

Buck pushed Pat forward and the giraffe stood beside Night awkwardly.

"Against the wall," Buck ordered.

Pat did so, and pressed to the wall beside Night.

"No, pussy. In front of her!"

Pat side-stepped in front of Night, who briefly lifted an arm off the wall to let him pass. She smirked and slowly shook her head. "My goofy boy," she crooned.

The rhino casually slapped her ass—setting seismic ripples through her richly proportioned body. Night whimpered, her eyes going ever so slightly out of focus with eager lust as the rhino gripped her tail at the base and used it to lift her up, making her moan and press her muzzle against Pat's belly. Normally, this posture would feel intimate. Close. But Night felt a million miles away—and Pat knew there was no one to blame but himself.

The rhino started to press into her. Night bared her teeth, her fingers crooking, her nails drawing thin white lines against the porcelain walls of the shower. Pat trembled, and his hand tugged his shorts down to let his cock finally spring free. He started to work his member slowly, pumping himself as he watched Night's eyes slowly close to slits. It *was* Night, wasn't it? It wasn't all an act, surely? She was clearly delighting in this.

Pretense and act felt like it had fallen away and Pat's heart hammered as he had to imagine that cock sliding into her—inch by inch, spreading her wider. And then, as if a dam had broken, the rhino suddenly pushed forward. His balls slapped against her belly, his hips meeting hers with a meaty *thock*.

Night cried out. It wasn't coherent, just sounds as if she had forgotten how to form words.

Her hands skidded along the wall, to Pat's shoulders, to his chest. Her fingers twisted up his shirt, lifting it, allowing the tips of her nails to press against his bare fur. She clenched her sharp nails against Pat's stomach, while the rhino jackhammered into her. His hips slammed against her rump again and again, his balls pounding her belly with an audible *plap plap plap*. Her breasts swayed in delicious counterpoint to his thrusts and her drool dripped onto Pat's belly as he leaned back and away from her and the rhino, trying to sink into the wall. His hand worked his cock faster and faster and he gritted his teeth. A desperate whine escaped his lips as the

rhino paused in his thrusting just long enough to adjust his grip, realign Nights hips with her tail, and then go back to hammering away at her.

"He's fucking *destroying* me..." Night groaned, her eyes closed to slits as she looked up at Pat, mashing her breasts against him. "I'm getting fucked by a stranger, and he's *ruining* my cunt," she gasped.

"Fucking right I am," the rhino said with a grin. He took a quick step forward, pausing in his thrusting to press Night against Pat even more. Her cum-soaked breasts slipped against his chest, her hard nipples prodding his skin through his fur. The rhino began to fuck her again, driving her into Pat. Her nose was pressed nearly against his, her breath hot against his face and she moaned wordless pleasure.

Night's lips were close to Pat's, but she never tried to kiss him. There was too much distance between them—between her, the beautiful mistress, and him, the pathetic cuck. His body trembled and he felt his long delayed orgasm burn through him. His cum spurted from his cock, splashing against the underside of her breasts, soaking her fur as the rhino grinned over her shoulder at him, his horn glinting as he shifted his head back. His lips skinned back even more as his jaw tightened in effort. He was getting close to his climax.

Night shuddered and ducked her head forward. The violent reaction made Pat jerk back and slide downward, to where he was resting on his rear. Now with a clearer view of what was going on, he saw the rhino's heavy cock swing around between Night's trembling, cum-streaked legs.

The rhino groaned. "F-Fuck! Bitch squeezed me right out."

Pat looked up to see Night looking down at him, her eyes glowing with lust. He glanced back to see the thick cock, glistening with her juices, grinding against her belly as the rhino thrust his hips as if he were still inside her; as if his muscles hadn't quite caught up to the reality of the situation.

There was the patter of footsteps, and Pat could see the legs of both Buck and the otter walk around either side of them.

"Hungry for more?" came Buck's familiar voice.

Pat looked up and saw Night turning and wasting no time taking Buck's long member back into her mouth. She pumped him with a hand, shaking saliva loose to rain down on Pat. Then a brown hand reached over and the otter, stroking his long cock, pushed his semi-hard member at her. She gingerly suckled it into her mouth like a noodle, coaxing it back to rigidity.

She went back and forth between the two cocks, getting the men hard again. All the while, Pat watched meekly from below, the perspective obscuring the men's faces as their cocks and balls blocked most of his view.

"I think we can get another couple loads ready for her," Buck purred.

"Fuck, I'm game for when the rhino's done," the otter laughed. "I've never seen a bird this hungry, especially for a gent my age." As if to drive home the point, he turned her head abruptly off Buck's cock and slid the entirety of his own length into her, his belly once again blocking her nostrils. Being this close to the otter, Pat could now get a whiff of his body odor. Clearly he hadn't showered already after a hard day at the gym, and he reeked. The thought of an old, fat, smelly man getting to face fuck a woman as fine as Nightshade made Pat's ears grow hot in shame—especially since he found it so oddly arousing.

The rhino grunted, grabbed his cock, and then slammed back into Night. She pulled off the otter's cock and cried out, throwing her head back. Her knees quivered and she threw her hands down to clench onto Pat's shoulders for support as the rhino fucked her fiercely.

"God, Pat, he's so… big! I can't stop cumming," Night gasped as the rhino pounded away at her. His thrusts grew more rapid, his balls slapping against her clit, his large hands holding her tight as he thrust hard into her once, twice, three times—and then his own growl filled the air. It was an almost subsonic rumble, buzzing through Night's body. Her eyes widened and she let out a soft whine as the rhino grunted, each grunt accompanied by a deep thrust as his balls twitched, pumping load after load of fresh cum inside her.

For the second time that afternoon, a man had cum inside her. Pat could hear a soft pattering sound as the rhino's cum dripped from Night's pussy, flowing along his balls and falling to the floor below.

It felt like an eternity as the rhino kept grunting and twitching, and then finally, it ebbed away, and he tugged out of her, letting loose a torrent of cum that splashed onto the floor of the shower in a loud *splat*. Pat looked and saw Night's toes had curled, her thighs quaking, as she rode an orgasmic high. He could only imagine what the scene from the other side must look like, her ruined pussy a gaping orifice, stretched and painted white with cum.

His imaginings were cut short from the sound of the rhino smacking Night's ass, the sound akin to a gunshot.

"Best pussy I've ever had." The rhino's chuckle was cruel. "Shame you're not getting a shot at it, huh?" He looked down at Pat.

"She ready for another?" the otter interrupted, stroking himself impatiently.

Night's eyes went wide, and an expectant grin crossed her lips. Her eyes locked with Pat's, but he said nothing. Night nodded eagerly and Pat found any objections dying in his throat.

"Go wild," Buck mused.

There was a brief clicking sound as the otter's toenails scraped across the floor, and Pat looked ahead to see his legs position themselves behind Night's wondrous thighs. The otter's tail snaked back and forth as he fumbled with his cock, trying to slide it into the jackal, only to be deterred by the slick juices of the prior men. Finally, he found his destination, and easily slid balls deep inside her, sending a small torrent of cum spilling out of her by the new occupying cock.

"Ohh, blimey, this is intense," the otter bellowed as he thrust into her, his saggy balls flopping against her belly. Night groaned, her brow scrunched up as what Pat could only imagine was a mixture of pleasure and shame filled her. She took a hand off his shoulders and reached around her swinging breasts to stroke her clit as the otter pounded away at her.

"Your girl is a real slut, isn't she?" Pat heard a familiar voice ask. He broke his eyes away from the lurid sights before him to see Buck addressing him. "Two strangers. Not even in their prime." He turned to look at the otter. "No offense."

"None taken," the otter chuckled, his voice strained and was hardly audible over the wet sounds of his thrusting against Night's sloppy orifice.

Buck knelt down on one knee. His cock was perilously close to Pat's face. It was long, curved downward in a semi-hard state, having gone somewhat limp since Night took her focus off it. Pat could see every vein, even fold in the skin, and the smell—God, the smell of pure masculinity hit him like a shockwave. If it had this kind of effect on him, who knew what it did to Nightshade.

"After he's done, I'm going to fuck her brains out," Buck declared. It wasn't even a question or a theoretical. It was just a statement, as if he had an appointment on his busy calendar. Pat's eyes darted between Buck's eyes and his cock, which had begun to swell as the sadistic deer pelted him with admonishments. "And when I'm through, you can finally get your turn, like the little bitch you are."

Pat's ears perked up at the sound of Night moaning urgently. He turned his attention away from Buck—and Buck's cock—to see Night's wrists furiously rubbing between her thighs. Her body jerked and convulsed as she orgasmed. The otter was forced out of her as she crumpled to the ground, gasping and shaking in a heap, her head resting in Pat's lap.

Pat reached forward instinctively and turned her on her back, bringing his legs inward and crossing them to provide a perch to rest her head on. Night murmured, her eyes fluttering as her orgasm bloomed through her. She looked oddly at peace. But then the moment was broken as the otter knelt in front of her and pushed back her thick thighs. His access reacquired, he slid his cock back inside her and began grinding, using his shoulders to prop up her legs to allow for maximum penetration.

Night panted as the otter fucked her, each thrust pushing her head against Pat's lap—and cock. She threw her arms back to find Pat's wrists and held them firmly as the otter increased his tempo. Pat relished the support she sought from him; that small bond keeping him focused.

The otter leaned forward and suckled one of her nipples, then the other, and then trailed his way up her neck, his bristly mustache tickling her and getting strands of her long, raven-black hair caught up in it. Seeing she was panting, he sought out her tongue and took it into his own mouth, bits of his cum from earlier mixing with their saliva as he tongue played with her.

Pat winced at the sight, and then noticed Buck out of the corner of his eye. Now fully hard, he stood up and walked around to the side, slowly stroking himself as he waited his turn. It didn't take long, as just seconds later the otter buried his head into Nadia's neck and groaned as he thrust balls deep into her and came. His orgasm was noticeably shorter than the others, partly because he likely had little left in him after earlier, but it was enough to make Night softly whimper.

The otter pulled back and staggered as he made to stand. Buck assisted him upright and gave him a back pat of approval before taking his place.

He looked down almost lovingly at Night's pussy, which Pat could see was pooling cum around the floor. "Turn over, love. I want to get a view of that lovely arse of yours."

Obediently, Night turned over. Too weak—or the floor to slippery—to steady herself on all fours, she chose instead to lay flat on her stomach. Her nose bushed Pat's cock, and instinctively her tongue darted out to touch it.

"Heh, go ahead. Give your boy some attention. He's been patient today," Buck said, kneeling behind Night, cock in hand. Night obeyed and darted her tongue out again, this time letting it linger on Pat's cock, slowly, encouragingly, guiding it into her warm, wet maw. She suckled on it gingerly at first, then more steadily, rocking her head back and forth as she worshipped his shaft in her muzzle.

"Mmm, you're such a slut, aren't you?" Buck groaned, sliding his luridly thick cock back inside her with ease. The sudden sensation of being filled again made Night moan and let Pat's cock fall out of her mouth. She took it in a hand and urgently stroked it.

"Yes," Night said, her voice a desperate whimper as Buck began to fuck her, the sound of his hips meeting her juice-covered rump producing lurid, echoing smacking sounds.

"You'd take anyone's cock, wouldn't you? Even some beggar's off the street?"

Night tossed her head from side to side, rapturous in her shameful lust. "Yes!"

"I bet you'd fuck a whole room of guys, wouldn't you?" Buck hissed, pumping her faster, harder, revelling in the dirty talk. "You've done it before, like you told me… back in your old days."

"I would."

"And how you wanted to do it again."

"Yesss."

Buck's thrusts grew more urgent. His body rippled and crackled with energy as Nightshade continued to fiercely stroke Pat. Concern and shame slammed around in Pat's head as he imagined vivid scenarios. Night, like in her younger days, surrounded by men, fucked and pampered like a queen. So many men providing for her. More than Pat felt he could provide.

"How about we arrange that, hmm? I know plenty of fat cats who'd love to get a piece of you. You want that, huh? You want to get fucked by anyone who wants you?"

"I just want cock! Any cock will do!" Night gasped out around her moans.

"Any cock but his?" Buck sneered, his eyes suddenly meeting Pat's. They were cold, like ice.

"Any but his!" Night cried out.

That was the limit. Pat's balls tightened and cum jetted from his cock, splattering across Nightshade's face, hair, and ears. She opened her mouth in a happy pant as he painted her. If at one time she had been too proud for facials, that moment was long gone. Night lowered her head, shuddering and moaning as she gripped Pat's cock while cum still ebbed from it. Buck too moaned and jerked back, set off by Night's orgasm. He ground against inside her and pumped another hot load of cum deep inside. The fourth that day.

"Nnh, you fucking whore, take every last drop!" he bellowed, pinning her down and grinding her to the hilt, trying to milk everything he had into her insatiable orifice.

Night was flattened to the floor in a puddle of cum as Buck pushed and ground his crotch against her luscious buttcheeks, squishing and moving them as he painted every last corner of her insides white. When his orgasm finally waned, he pulled himself out, his long cock absolutely drenched in cum, then turned the sticky jackal over to face her, threads of silken semen trailing from her body to the floor.

In a surprising turn, Buck took her face in his hands and tenderly ran his tongue along hers before deeply kissing her. When their lips parted, he gazed into her eyes and whispered something to her that Pat couldn't make out. Nadia's eyes sparkled and she drew him in for another deep kiss. Somewhere in the thrusting—in the fucking—Pat had stopped thinking of her as Nightshade and instead seen Nadia, and that was the moment it dawned on him. He groaned in shame as his cock throbbed to half mast, spurred on by the jealousy of seeing the intimate bond Nadia was sharing with Buck—or was it Ezra?

"Good girl," Buck whispered. He then sat up, and turned to the two men behind him. "You can leave now gentlemen. Not a word of this to anyone, of course."

"Been a pleasure," the rhino said, flippantly waving. He threw a quick glance at Pat, and then turned and left. The otter, too, wandered off.

Buck turned and gave Nadia and Pat a slight nod, then stood. "I'm going to clean up and go as well. You should be a good little bitch and wash your woman before taking her home, Pat. That is, unless you *want* the whole of London to see your cock slut of a girlfriend do a cum walk." The tall cervine laughed to himself before disappearing around the corner, leaving Nadia and Pat suddenly alone.

"Did you enjoy that, Patty-Cakes?"

Pat blinked and looked down to see Nadia looking up at him. Her expression was a mixture of amusement and exhaustion. Her eyes were happy and half-lidded, shining through ropes of cum that adorned her face.

Pat thought of how to respond. He both loved and hated it. Which was sort of the point. The kink itself was a wild rollercoaster of emotions, of combative impulses. It was intoxicating. But regardless of that, at this moment he was happy and relieved that it was Nadia - not Nightshade, not Buck, nor anyone else - who was solely giving him attention.

"It was intense. How... how are you feeling, hon?"

Nadia laughed softly. "Me? That took me back..." She closed her eyes, then groaned. "God *damn*, I'm knackered though."

Pat wanted to laugh. Or maybe cry. Part of him felt as if he had just been in the sexiest, hottest thing in the universe. Another part was terrified of what it might mean for his future. For *their* future. Instead, he shook his head. "Can you even stand?" he asked, trying to sound casual.

Nadia nodded, then yawned slowly. "Yeah..." She closed her eyes, rolled her shoulders, then started to stand. "Oh! Oh! Ohhh!" She winced as she stretched out her knees, nearly falling over. Pat leapt to his feet and caught her, stabilizing her. She used his support to straighten her posture, then rolled her shoulders, popping sounds emanating throughout her body. "I'm going to have to lean on you while we clean up, Patty-Cakes."

Pat smiled. "That's what I'm here for."

They took a long, hot, wordless shower together, enjoying each other's company. Pat using the entirety of a bottle of shampoo and a bottle of conditioner to get the cum out of Nadia's fur. He took his time scrubbing her, smoothing out her fur, tracing his hands along her sleek, curvaceous body. Worshipping her. His mistress.

Only his?

That took me back.

The words echoed in his head. It was already intimidating being compared to Buck. But memories of Night's revelries in the years before she met Pat made him worry. Was he enough? Was this taste of her old life drawing her back? Buck was tempting enough, but what of the multitudes of opportunities a man with that much wealth and power could provide? It must have been so tempting for her. Pat had wanted to use the safeword, to stop this before that genie was let out of its bottle. But Nightshade had already been freed. For all he knew, it was already too late. Maybe it had *always* been too late.

And it was all his fault.

After showering and cleaning up, they took the tube home. Nadia fell asleep on his shoulder, leaving him to his own thoughts, which in a way were more tormenting than any roleplaying scenario. Pat felt like the whole transition from public to private took place in a blur, a blur of incoherent thoughts, guilt, excitement.

Once home, Nadia stripped and collapsed onto the bed, softly snoring almost as soon as her head hit the pillow. Pat gently tucked her in, and then took a step back to gaze at the peacefully snoozing jackal. All confusion and uncertainty felt like it had collapsed into a single fact.

Nadia really didn't need just *him* anymore, did she?

He knew what he had to do.

He quietly changed into street clothes, not wanting to wake Nadia up despite her being out like a light. He checked his phone and saw the weather report that it was beginning to rain. Grabbing a hoodie, he took one last look at Nadia, crept to the front door, and slipped into the gathering storm.

CHAPTER 9

"I'm sure some of you are already wanting to reach into the past and smack me. Don't worry. Someone did."

* * *

Pat felt like he had been walking for hours—in a daze. His feet knew where he was going, even if he didn't. It actually took himself a few moments to realize that he was standing before a door. He shook himself, trying to focus. He was here. Now he just had to…knock.

He lifted his hand.

The door to the flat opened and Pat found himself nose-to-nose with weaponized adorability. He blinked slowly as he looked into the wide eyes of an incredibly short red panda. Her tail was almost as long as she was, and she demonstrated it by bundling it against her flat, petite chest and burying her nose against its soft bushiness. Her hair was dark amber and framed her face perfectly. Something that could have marred her cuteness—a pair of bulky, yellow work gloves—nestled between the fur. They were caked with signs of hard work and love; thick mud and bits of dirt that mixed with the fur.

"Hey Ruby," Pat said, trying to sound his normally goofy, cheery self, dropping his arm and tucking it behind his back. He knew that Ruby was shy, after all.

Ruby inclined her head, then stepped backwards. She buzzed around the corner of the entrance corridor so fast that she almost left behind a blur in the air.

A clattering of hooves and a skidding sound presaged the arrival of Glitter. Nadia's boss did not look how she normally did. Most of the time when Pat had seen her, Glitter was the picture of a professional. She had been the one to set him up on a blind date with Nadia, back when Pat had thought of the jackal as an elegant and enticing yet seemingly unapproachable bitch-slash-ice-queen-slash-*oh-my-god-that-amazing-ass* type of girl. Glitter's normal ensemble was a sharp suit, nice skirt, and professional little eyeglasses—a look somewhere between mob boss and high school principal. And yet she exuded a kind of sensual allure that made her seem more exotic than either of those things.

Her horns didn't exactly hurt. She was a gazelle; orange-gold fur along her edges, with a pearl white color for her hands, belly. Breasts. Pat tried to not think about those as he looked at Glitter... well... at Vicky. Her real name was Victoria, and it was easier to think of her as a Vicky here at her home. She was dressed in a low-hanging t-shirt that left what seemed like an acre-and-a-half of her chest and shoulders exposed. It hung down around her thighs, making it hard to tell if she was even wearing shorts. Long, lean calves were on display, and her hooves clicked on the ground softly.

"Patrick?" she said, sounding slightly confused. "What brings you here, in this weather?"

Pat opened his mouth, then saw Ruby. She was hiding around the corner, her eyes gleaming with clear curiosity. She might not have been asking questions, but she definitely wanted to have them answered. If she noticed him noticing her, she gave no sign of it. Vicky, though, seemed to know her girlfriend's mind better than Pat knew his own. She grinned.

"Let's head to my room. And get that soaking hoodie off before you flood the place."

The door to her room shut and Pat rubbed his hands along his snout. The hoodie was heavy with moisture. Taking it off felt great, though he noticed that the dampness had gotten through to soak his undershirt as well. He was glad to be in a heated room. The white fabric of his undershirt clung to his chest. Vicky looked at him with concern, her hands clasping together as she regarded him.

"You must have almost caught your death out there," she said, shaking her head. "I would've thought by now you would be prepared for handling London weather."

Pat brushed his hands through his wet hair as Vicky sat on her bed and crossed her legs underneath her, folding them taut and adjusting her shirt to reach out over her knees. It created a tent that made her look almost shapeless, like a pretty gazelle head set on top a trapezoidal tank.

"Well, um..." Pat rubbed his shoulder, not sure where to begin.

Vicky was like a mother hen to the girls at the Safari, and ran a clean, tight ship. She was more than a boss, she was their confidant, and she had been Nadia's best friend for many years, even if she never let that friendship get in the way of cracking the whip at the Safari. It was her wisdom and knowledge that drew Pat here. She had often advised him in the past, but now he needed it more than ever.

"Is it something between you and Nadia?" Vicky asked, her voice serious.

"No!" Pat said, quickly. "Nadia and I are…" Ugh. He was already lying again. He had gotten so reflexively used to saying that things were fine that he was doing it even with Vicky now. He shook his head, slightly. "Yes." Saying it aloud felt like a physical blow.

Vicky's eyes widened. "You didn't…" she paused, then shook her head. "You didn't ruin all my hard work, did you?"

"What?" Pat asked, baffled.

"I set you two up, silly," Vicky said, arching an eyebrow. "I don't want to see my matchmaking go up in flames or anything."

Pat shook his head. "No, it's not *that*. We're not… well… maybe it is." He sighed, rubbing his hands through his hair. "I… I don't even know where to begin."

"At the beginning?" Vicky suggested, her brow furrowing slightly.

Pat chuckled. "That would be the place to start. Okay. Um. How frank should I get?"

"Well, I run the Safari, I think I can handle PG-13 at least," Vicky said.

Pat tried to lighten his mood: "Don't you mean 12A?" he asked.

Vicky giggled. "I was translating for you, Yank," she said, shaking her head. "Come on. Spill." She slipped her hand out from under the hem of her shirt to pat the bed next to her. Pat stood and then walked over and sat next to her.

Pat sighed as he felt the warmth of the room and the concern in her voice fill him. It made him feel comforted. Wanted. Something that he wasn't sure he'd ever feel with Nadia again. Not after the gym. That was the final nail in the coffin, wasn't it? And he couldn't even say didn't like it, because he was a sick, sick freak.

Pat shook his head, trying to get his brain on a single track. "Have you ever heard of cuckolding?"

"Yes," Vicky said, seriously. "Nadia knows it too, since she used to be a domme. She was good at that sort of thing. Teasing men. That's why I hired her, after all. And I'm not *entirely* shocked you're into it, Pat. There's a reason you were attracted to her in the first place. No offense."

Rain pattered against the window, and in the distance, thunder rumbled. Pat gulped.

"Yeah," he said. "Well we've been exploring it. A-And it's been thrilling. But I think it went too far, and I worry she's grown bored of me. You know, like she might want to return to her glory days, before she met me? I... I'm afraid she's settling with me, and she's realizing it."

Vicky clicked her tongue. "You think she's tempted by other men?"

Pat sighed and rubbed his eyes. "We were having a scene with our bull... well, he's not *literally* a bull, but you know what I mean. And then others joined it. It was exhilarating in how wrong it was, but seeing her give herself to them like that... I didn't know what I wanted. I considered using the safeword. Nadia *told* me that the thing she hated most in the world was a domme who failed to live up to a safeword. I didn't use it and I put her in that position."

He thought for a second, as the sound of rain echoed in the room. "I... I told her it was okay. And it wasn't. *I* was not okay, and I didn't tell her." He shook his head, his hair flipping out, splashing Vicky with some flecks of rain. "But even if I had said the safeword..." He sighed, hanging his head forward. "T-There's a reason I didn't say it, Vicky. She's enjoying herself too much. I don't want to ruin this for her. But I'm also terrified of her leaving me. Especially since our bull... deer... he's bigger than me. A lot bigger. And insanely confident and masculine a-and he even has real antlers! And I've *never* seen Nadia happier in my life."

Vicky shook her head. "Have you spoken to Nadia about this?" She asked.

Pat rubbed his palms along his face. He felt his muzzle start to burn as his hands caressed along his head, catching on his ossicones. He worked his memory back through the last evening, and felt his stomach turn slowly over. He groaned quietly.

"N-No," Pat admitted. He could already see that he had made the biggest mistake of his life. Or, at the very least, one of them.

"Patrick Patel!" Vicky said, her voice firm, rolling out his full name like a school marm. "You're telling me that you didn't *talk* to her before coming here?"

Pat stood up quickly. He flushed hard, trying to stammer out a few excuses. They stumbled out of his mouth, but he stopped himself before he even got past the first word. Sometimes, the first syllable.

"B-But what if- that is, I… uh, no, that is, um, I… well…" Pat started again and again. "I… Ezra Maes is-"

Vicky shook her head and jerked back, almost slamming her horns into the wall. "Wait, you're being cucked by Ezra *Maes*? The guy on Star Talk!? The *billionaire?*"

"M-Multibillionaire, actually," Pat said, remembering having his nose ground into that fact. "That's just it, though! He's like me! But unlike me, he's rich and he's hung and he's insanely confident. H-He makes Nadia *submissive!* Her! How the fuck could she ever want me again after him?"

Vicky scowled. "Patrick. Patrick. *Patrick.* Don't you dare… I… " She clenched her fists, as if he had insulted her. Then she breathed out all her anger, her hands unwinding as she sat up. Her eyes closed and she spoke like a drill instructor: "What's Nadia's most sensitive erogenous zone?"

"Ears," Pat said, without thinking.

"Favorite video game?"

"Doesn't have one, she reads instead," Pat said, his tail swishing back and forth.

"Favorite author?"

"Clive Barker," Pat said, nodding.

"Place to visit?" Vicky cocked an eyebrow as she opened one eye.

"Castles and cemeteries," he said. "She likes gothic, historical sites. Her favorite chocolate is darker than her fur. She takes her steak rare, her back rubs hard, and… holy shit, I know a lot of details…" He blinked slowly.

"That's because she *lets* you know that stuff," Vicky said. "You two got set up for a reason! I'm not bad at this matchmaking stuff, you know, and I'm bloody insulted that you doubted me, honestly." She stuck her tongue out at him. "You're the kind of person who would know… who would know a band she secretly loves!"

"The Bangles," Pat said, still in answering mode.

Vicky smiled. "See, I didn't even know that." She stood up and walked over to Patrick, reaching out and placing her palm on his cheek. Her voice was soft. "You said, earlier, that she has never been happier. But you didn't know her *before* you. And I can tell you, Nadia's had quite the life. She's been worshipped, cherished, fucked silly in orgies. But I've known her long before you arrived, and I can tell you she's never been happier than she is now. Even the past week she always talks about you at work. She never once brought up Ezra Maes. Not a hint."

She slid her hand away from Pat. "She's happier with you. Trust me. She's a smart girl and knows this is a fun diversion. Don't doubt what you have with her. And most of all…" Her finger thrust to the door. "Go and *talk* to her. Tell her how you feel. Be honest. Figure this *out*."

Pat nodded, picked up his hoodie, then turned for the door. He opened it and found Ruby trying to sneak away from the keyhole she had been listening through. Pat frowned at her. She grinned, shyly, then held up her gloved hands. Pat's frown lightened and then he smiled, leaned forward and kissed her at the top of her head.

"You have a good girlfriend," he said.

Ruby nearly fainted.

CHAPTER 10

"So, advice for anyone in a similar position as mine: The truth will always, always, always hurt less than a lie. Both in the short term and in the long."

* * *

Pat drew in deep gasps as he ran—and yet, despite the fact he was sprinting through the rain, he felt like he was flying. His shoes rasped on the pavement as he ran, a huge, goofy smile splitting his face.

He made Nadia happy.

He did it.

He could fix this. He could fucking fix this, he knew he could. He came to the flat, then started up the stairs, taking them five steps at a time, leaping up and up, until he was at the door. He lifted his hand to knock, water dripping from his soaked fur.

The door opened and Patrick was suddenly holding an armful of Nadia. She clung to him, then drew back, her voice holding a touch of Scottish brogue that she normally kept under her cosmopolitan persona. "Where the *bloody* hell have you been, you clod?" She nuzzled his neck, licking him fiercely. "I thought you got mugged! Your phone was off and-"

"It was off?" Pat blinked, and then pulled the phone from his hoodie pocket.

Turns out that his hoodie didn't protect from water nearly enough. The phone was bricked. Pat looked at it, feeling like he had gone full circle for some reason. He tossed it aside casually, not caring about it one iota.

"Nadia…" he drew in a slow breath. He had to get this out. He could do it—even if his earlier confidence felt like it was getting a bit shakier. "I'm sorry."

"You better be sorry, or have a bloody good reason…" Nadia shook her head, then dragged him across the room. She set him down on the sofa, stripped him naked, and had him covered in a blanket before Pat could get a single word out. She made him stay and warm up while she used an electric kettle to make him a cup of piping hot tea with a spoonful of honey and a single mint leaf, just how he liked it. She had it in his hands moments later. With her giraffe properly tended to, she finally sat down beside him and looked straight into his eyes.

"So," she began. "What happened?"

Pat paused. "I… I wanted to but… didn't use the safeword. At the gym. I lied. W-when I said I was okay.""

Nadia blinked, and slowly drew in her breath, as if death itself had touched her. "Oh…"

Pat shook his head. "And, rather than talking to you about it, I went for a big, sulky walk in the rain, to go get advice from Vicky."

Nadia looked harrowed. She lowered her head, ears pinned back as her bangs covered her eyes. "This is my fault."

"It is not!" Pat exclaimed, setting the cup down to free his hands up.

Nadia shook her head. "Oh, but it is. I know you, Pat." She rubbed her temples, looking stressed. "I let Buck play the dom role, but he's not experienced enough. I should have been paying more attention. I-" She shook her head, while Pat leaned into her. His nose pressed to her neck and he drew her into a hug.

"No," he murmured. "I should have been honest. Admittedly I *did* enjoy it, but I grew worried. I was feeling it was becoming overwhelming."

Nadia closed her eyes and reached up with her hand. Her fingers pressed against the softness of his neck. She petted him as she continued. "I… I have been wondering if things were going too far, despite you saying no limits. You're such a chatterbox, I thought you'd let me know if you were bothered. But I should've listened to that gut instinct." Her eyes closed and she leaned in closer. "I'm really sorry Pat. I got carried away and let it get out of control."

Pat opened his mouth to respond, but stopped himself. They could circle each other, apologizing and taking the blame for hours, but never get to the root of the issue. While he knew that he was more at fault for not voicing his concerns, would Nadia ever accept that? And what would that gain them? His hands shifted from her shoulders to her hips, sliding along her body in a slow, loving sweep. He dragged Nadia fully onto his lap and sighed.

"I don't want anyone to be blamed for this, even if I feel it's my fault."

He grinned as her head ducked forward while she leaned into him. "What *really* matters... what I want most? I want you to know that I realized... I never really told you. Like, *really* told you, that I love you, Nadia. I love you so... so much." He shook his head. "A-And I was scared, and I know I shouldn't have been. I know I should trust you."

Nadia looked on quizzically as Pat continued. "I want you to be happy, and I love seeing you enjoy yourself. I think of how lucky I am to be with you. I still don't know why you're with a guy like me." He ran his fingers along the edge of her ear. "But I have it on good authority that you *are* happy. Even if I can't offer you the things someone like Ezra can."

He sighed. He reached out and picked up the tea cup, realizing he should drink it before it grew cold. Pat gazed down at the steam drifting from the cup in his hands. "This evening, I felt like I saw the *old* Nightshade, the one who lived like a queen, with men at her beck and call. I wanted to see that side of you, but then I wondered, what could I *possibly* bring to the relationship at this point? What started off as kinky roleplay has really made me fear that I may lose you, Nadia." He paused, seeing her expression. Nadia was looking thoughtful.

It was the playful, teasing thoughtful. The kind that made Pat feel more relief than anything he could have imagined—it was the subtle grin of Nadia about to tease him. He relaxed back as Nadia reached up and caressed his cheek once more. "Patrick... do you know how many calories are in a quart of cum?" she asked.

Pat blinked. He had braced for some serious teasing. He had not been prepared for *that* kind of a response. He opened his mouth, closed it, and then managed to say: "Buzhwaah?"

"A tenth of a percent of a single calorie," Nadia said, nodding seriously. "Don't ask me how I know that, but it's less nutritionally filling than cardboard."

"How do-" Pat started, grinning. Nadia snapped her teeth right under his nose and Pat laughed.

"Do you know how many lasses and lads have this fantasy of *living* on cum?" Nadia shook her head. "Even I've had my moments, when I would find someone with a really nice musk and a great taste." She smiled. "But a lass can't live on cum, Patrick. Buck? Buck is cum. You? You're a five course meal with a backrub."

Pat laughed, ruefully. "Wow."

Nadia grinned. "And if you want..." Her grin faded. "We can break this off with Buck. You can say your safeword at any time, and it's over. No hurt feelings, no guilt."

Pat chuckled. "I dunno, you *do* have so much fun with him," he said, his eyes sparkling as he looked down at Nadia—and he saw that tension was bleeding out of her as well. She had been, in her own roundabout way, trying to unburden him. Now, he could see her letting her own tension slide away. It was as if their relationship was rebalancing—shifting the center of gravity to be lower to the ground. More stable.

"True," she said, shrugging one shoulder.

"And you get so *submissive* around him," Pat murmured.

"Drives you batty, doesn't it?" Nadia chuckled. "Remember I can play roles, too. It's fun to play the cock slut, especially with how much it makes you squirm. Part of my training as a domme was to get dommed by others, you know? I couldn't possibly be submissive all the time, though. It's just not in my nature."

"So that was all an act?" Pat asked. "It seemed really genuine."

Nadia's ears flicked and she seemed to blush. "Well, I can't say I don't get a *bit* into the role. Buck's rather… intoxicating. I can't help but indulge myself a little. But even so…"

Nadia bit her lip in thought.

"When I was a domme, I wore a mask," she said. "When I work at the Safari, I wear a mask. When I'm with Buck, or even Ezra, I wear a mask. We had a nice, polite conversation when I first visited him at the office. Ezra was talking about possible future scenes, but I never stopped being calculating, aloof Nightshade, even with him in private." She lifted her chest, putting her hand to her collarbone, mockingly imitating this version of her.

Pat blinked, thinking of the moments where the two had whispered and laughed with each other privately. "But you two seemed so… in tune after the sex. When he's Ezra, not Buck, that is."

Nadia shrugged. "Well… yeah? We do have some chemistry. I'm obviously not going to do all this with a bloke I don't get along with. But us having a laugh doesn't mean I'm going to run off with him, silly."

Pat shook his head. Suddenly all his worries seemed so trivial and ridiculous.

"The point is, I'm not the real me when I'm at the Safari. I'm not the real me when I'm with Buck. The 'old Nightshade' isn't even truly me. Those are personas." Nadia leaned forward and her emerald eyes softened as she gazed into Pat's. "You're the only one who has ever really seen the person behind the mask. You know Nadia, not just Nightshade. Ezra isn't allowed to know the real me."

Nadia took one of Pat's hands and kissed it. "I love you, Patty-Cakes. What we have is genuine. It's a feeling that doesn't happen with others. I'm not leaving you, I promise. Especially not for some hotshot businessman."

Pat relaxed into the sofa. "So, we're good." He smiled. "Though, just to check: The fact he's rich…"

Nadia snorted, rolling her eyes. "Please. I'm not a gold digger, Pat."

"And he's going into space," Pat added, grinning. He felt weak with relief, like he had sprinted for miles.

Nadia chuckled. "I don't want to go to bloody *Mars*."

"He's not even going to Mars!" Pat laughed.

"Whatever." Nadia shrugged one shoulder, then parted the blanket to lay against his chest. She closed her eyes and murmured. "You take me further anyway, Patrick."

Pat reached over and gently caressed her head. His fingers stroked through her raven-black hair. "I'm sorry I let my insecurities get to me. I just think so highly of you, and I never got what you see in me."

"Ah," Nadia said, lifting a finger to make a point. "You can respect me, and admire me. You can even worship me to a degree, but *don't* put me on a pedestal. I'm not infallible." She snuggled tightly to Pat, breathing in his scent. "And don't worry about other men. You're my first 'normal' relationship, and you'd be surprised how adventurous that can be in its own way."

"Even if I'm holding you back?"

"Pfft, holding me back!" Nadia laughed. "Pat, believe me. You're not. I think we both know who wears the trousers in this relationship."

"Well I'm not wearing the skirt, that's for sure," Pat said, chuckling. "Maybe I could try for a kilt."

Nadia smiled and gave him a wink. "I'd approve of that."

Pat silently stroked Nadia's hair for a while. A wry smile crossed his face as he thought of something to break up the seriousness of the conversation. "So, uh, since we've been trying new stuff… can I put it in your butt?"

Nadia snorted. "Can I put mine in yours?"

Pat paused. Ever since they had started that little running gag, he had reacted with horror and fear—mostly exaggerated. But there was a core of real fear, at having his ass taken. Pat had always thought to himself: *Pfft,*

I'm not homophobic! I just don't think I'd like it in the butt. Still, he knew she wanted to peg him badly. But he wasn't ready to add more onto his quest list just yet.

"Maybe," he said, his voice soft. "If you get me *very* drunk."

"Mmm," Nadia purred. "Noted."

Pat sighed. He clicked his tongue, and then a lurking thought rushed back to him. "Wait, planning scenes?" he asked.

Nadia laughed softly. "What, did you think that I just *happened* to have sex with Buck in a locker room that just *happened* to have two eager-to-please gentlemen waiting and ready to go? Ezra found them. Even paid for their gym memberships." Her eyes glittered as she spread her hands along Pat's belly. "And Lily? Do you think any lass would go to work in a skirt that short, without knickers, not having *some* idea of what's coming? Or cumming, in your case." She nipped at him, gently.

Pat laughed. "Wow. So, *all* of that was planned?"

"Mmhmm," Nadia murmured, nuzzling his belly with her nose. "That's half the work of a dom, planning scenes."

Pat cleared his throat, feeling his cheeks flush. "I was so concerned about… doing it with Lily. I thought I was overstepping my bounds. Like I said before, it was fun but concerning."

Nadia looked up at Pat with a sly smile. "I figured if I was getting something extra, you should too. Lily didn't object." Her eyes glanced sideways and her brows furrowed. "Though, I *was* annoyed when she tried to hit on you afterwards. Lass needs to learn her boundaries." Her nails tightened ever so slightly against Pat's belly.

"So all those times you were seeing Ezra privately…?" Pat inquired.

"Besides getting to know each other, we spent a great deal of time planning scenes." Nadia nodded. "Those phone calls? The dinner? Meeting him at his office? We talked at length about what to do. How to slowly escalate the tension, how to play with your expectations. It was all about you, Patty-Cakes."

Pat blushed. He suddenly felt like a giant spotlight was shining down on him.

"W-Well I feel stupid."

"Don't," Nadia mused. "You weren't supposed to know. It would've taken the thrill out of it, ruined the illusion of spontaneity. I'm kicking myself for making it *too* unexpected, however."

Pat thought for a moment. About the rhino and the otter. Strangers taking turns fucking her in public. Ezra must've screened them. It was doubtful they'd see them again. Did Nadia even want to? Pat wanted to inquire. "D-Did it feel good to remember being the old, carefree Nightshade? Like at the gym...?"

"Yes and no," she whispered. "It's fun to indulge. To roleplay. That's what a lot of my domme days were like, you know. Discovering someone's kinks, thinking up a script. Acting out the scene in the safety of my planning, with the safeword as an emergency escape. I... admit I didn't realize how much I missed it." She bit her lip. "Plus, the sex is *really* amazing."

Pat gulped. He realized he hadn't drank his tea yet. He took a sip, and the minty, honeyed warmth filled his senses. "That's a big reason why I wanted to explore this. I wanted to see you in your element."

Nadia chuckled, her tone becoming more sultry. "Oh, this is child's play compared to the things I used to do. But you're not into whips and knives and the like. No, my little giraffe bruises too easily," she said, playfully giving him another nip—this one much harder.

Pat nearly spilled his tea. He remembered when they had first started dating, how Nadia's predatory side was more prominently on display. She had mellowed out since then, but their early explorations in the bedroom led to Pat discovering the limits of how deep her claws and fangs could go. "Y-Yeah, I'm not as into the pain stuff," Pat said. "At least, not physically."

Nadia softly licked the area she had nipped. "No, you like to be put into dilemmas. Scenarios. I've found your interests lie in psychological torture, not physical." She sat up, brushing her hair over her shoulder. "You're a writer. An intellectual. This is your way of working through your troubles."

She looked off at nowhere in particular. "I have mine, too, of course. Back when I was a domme, I tried everything. I didn't really know where I was going. What I'd be doing in my thirties. If I'd ever find a home." She settled back against Pat. "I think I've got it figured out now."

Pat closed his eyes, his fingers slipping once again through Nadia's beautiful hair. They remained there for a few moments—heartbeats that seemed to last forever.

"You did you still want to keep doing this?" came a soft inquiry. "Do you still trust me?"

Pat thought of responding in a joking manner, but thought now wasn't the time. "I *do* trust you," he replied. "And I want to continue this. As long as you're there with me."

Nadia squeezed his hand and then burrowed her snout into the crook of his arm. Time passed as they cuddled together. Pat took a sip of the tea and realized it was cold. He carefully leaned over and put it on the coffee table.

"So, shall I put on something romantic?" Pat finally asked, revelling in the lightness of being that had come over him. This past week had been a steady, painful crawl through delights and nightmares, and finding that the ending was a happy one had left him almost noodle-limp. Nadia murmured something that could have been a yes, her snout pressed against the side of Pat's chest. Her nose rubbed against his arm, then found his armpit, and she breathed him in. Pat blinked slowly.

"Are you smelling my armpit?"

"Nope," she drawled.

Pat shrugged, then groped around for the correct member of the family of remote controls they had collected over the years. Each sound system and TV came with a new one, and they all worked together in arcane ways. Pat found what he thought was the correct one as Nadia continued to rub against him. His free hand caressed her hair, petting her gently. Then he tapped down on the control and turned on the music with a wicked grin. A dance track started to thump from the speakers: *The Bad Touch* by the Bloodhound Gang filled the room with its goofy lyrics.

Nadia drew her head back. Her ears flicked back against her head and she gave Pat a dark, complex look; a look that reminded Pat of her preferred choice in coffee—blacker than midnight on a moonless night. Pat started to bob his head along with the music, grinning impishly at her. The verse for the song came on and he started to make tiny circles with his arms, dancing on the sofa in the most herbivore-ish way imaginable. Nadia, trying to keep the growing smile off her face, stood up and slowly began to roll her hips from side to side while watching him.

"Yeah!" Pat snapped his fingers in time with the music and stood as well. He felt three times dorkier when dancing next to Nadia, especially since he was naked. She was a trained dancer. Pole, strip, burlesque, ballroom. She could do all of them, though she was better at some than others. But rather than going into any of those patterns, she instead lifted her hands up, drawing her hands across her face as she rocked her hips from side to side. She went straight into *Walk Like an Egyptian*—a style as out of fashion as it was utterly dorky.

The verse started again as Pat did the robot, mechanically bumping his hip against Nadia's. She laughed, then grabbed his wrists and dragged him close. Her nose and his bumped together as the song slowly came to an end, the outro music repeating again and again, softer and softer each time.

"You are such a bad person, Pat," Nadia murmured.

"Just wait for the rest of the playlist," Pat whispered back.

The next song game on.

"*What is love!*" The speakers wailed.

Nadia growled, laughed, and shoved Pat back onto the sofa all at the same time. A moment later, she had pinned her rump down onto his thighs and had her hands on his shoulders. She leaned forward and hissed softly. "Just for that, I'm going to be *extra* cruel later."

Then she leaned forward and her tongue plunged into his mouth. Her hands grabbed his hair, tugging it hard until their lips broke contact. As Pat panted, Nadia leaned down, pushing his legs apart to expose his semi-hard cock that rested against his thigh. She snorted quietly as Nightshade mode returned. "You call *this* a dick?" she whispered, her voice hot as her hand closed around his member, which grew all the harder. She pumped him, her eyes glittering as she looked up at his face. "I won't even feel this, after getting so used to Buck. But maybe if you're willing to use your tongue, I *might* let you stick this tiny prick in me. How does *that* sound, giraffe boy?"

Pat grinned, widely.

And never once, not during the whole night, did he think of the word *Rutabaga*.

CHAPTER 11

"That, I think, is the real test of trying a kink like this. It's not just will you enjoy it, because if you don't, it'll end reflexively. You will end it, in fact, before any of the risks or dangers come up. The real test is finding out how to keep your fantasy separate from your life. That takes frequent, open communication and commitment. And I was going to learn it takes effort from more than just one person."

* * *

"Oh, Buck wants to talk to you," Nightshade said, rubbing her finger along her muzzle, making sure her fur was laid perfectly. The ring on her finger glinted in the sunlight. Night seemed to delight in drawing Pat's attention to it. Having her hands near her face did just that. Pat blushed and squirmed, and kept looking over his shoulder. The two of them were standing near the water fountain tucked into the corner of a large shopping center about ten minutes away from their flat.

Buck, making good on his promise to get Night some new panties after ruining two of her pairs, had invited them there. He had told Night to wear something nice, and so she was wearing a flowing black blouse paired with a tight skirt that was just short enough to make people imagine interesting things about her, while not being so short as to seem impractical. Buck had told Pat—with a wicked smirk and knowing gleam in his eyes—to bring lots of tote bags. Pat held those bags, feeling more servant than boyfriend, as Nightshade insisted he check her eye makeup.

"It looks good, right?" she asked. "I want to be pretty for my lover."

Pat gulped. "I-I, uh, I like it!"

He knew it was the wrong answer, but in the same way a pain slut talks back to their domme, he didn't care. Night snorted quietly, and put her finger against his nose, the glinting ring on it shimmering in the sunlight that shone through the skylights that gave the shopping center its airy, outdoor character.

"*Your* opinion doesn't matter. Do you think *Buck* will like it," Night murmured, her voice playful and chilly at the same time.

Pat's Adam's apple bobbed.

"Y-Yeah," he whispered, voice husky. "I think, um, I think Buck will love it."

Night nodded curtly. "Come along, then."

She led him to where Buck had asked to meet—the food court. There were a few garish fast food signs and a few more upscale places spread about. Buck, wearing a white polo shirt and khaki shorts that showed off his muscular form, was lounging beside a shady outcropping of greenery used to separate the tables meant for the more upscale places. His fingers plucked a leaf from the green and he popped it into his mouth, despite sitting within ten feet of a sign that said *Please Do Not Eat the Plants*. He chewed and watched as Patrick and Nightshade approached.

Pat was already half hard.

They stepped up to the table and Buck nodded at Night as she sat down next to him. The two of them kissed, tongues meeting as their muzzles locked. Buck's hand cupped and squeezed Night's thigh under the table as Pat sat there, blushing hard. He looked away from them—the noises just as erotic and shameful as watching them—and saw that, a few seats over, a young armadillo sitting with his parents was watching, eyes wide as saucers. His mother slapped the back of his head, and the armadillo coiled up in shock.

"So, bitch," Buck said, and Pat realized that the buff deer was talking to him. He looked over and blushed as Buck sneered. "Night here says you tried to fuck her last night?"

Pat blushed. "I-"

"She said she had to ask if you had gotten it in her," Buck said, casually.

"Wh-" Pat started again.

"Twice," Buck said, tilting his head to angle his antlers at him.

Pat flushed so hard that he was sure his spots were invisible. He closed his mouth, knowing that any more stammering would just make him look weaker. Of course, sitting there and taking Buck's abuse was also pretty weak. Both got him hard. His conscious mind drew backwards and he wallowed in the feeling of the moment; of powerlessness and humiliation, of knowing that if anyone walked by, they might hear and guess at what was going on.

"So, is that true?" Buck asked.

Pat nodded jerkily.

"Sorry, I didn't hear that," Buck said, not looking at him; he was busy gazing at Night. His eyes dipped and he casually, obviously ogled her tits. Night, rather than looking annoyed, giggled and shifted herself, pushing her chest outwards. "Mmm, your girl has a fine pair. Tell me Night, you ever going to let him see these again?"

"Only if you're the one tearing my clothes off me," Night whispered, her voice soft, but not soft enough. Pat heard it and tensed as she continued. "You're an *animal* in bed, Buck. You can fuck like an actual man."

"Fucking right I can," Buck said. "Pencil-dick, you still haven't answered my question."

Pat stammered. "I-I... s-she wasn't... sure if I was in her."

Buck sneered. "Because...?"

Pat hunched his shoulders, and under the table, his palm pressed against his cock in his pants. The pressure of clothes against him, restraining him, took his breath away. The fact that only a thin layer of fabric and his own posture hid his arousal from the people walking by made his heart pound. Buck leaned forward, cocking one ear, clearly wanting to hear the confession said louder. Pat leaned forward and huffed.

"B-Because you ruined her pussy," he said.

"And that means...?" Buck inquired.

Pat swallowed. "That I can't please her anymore."

Buck nodded. "Right you are. In fact, I'm thinking that before we go on this little shopping spree, I take her behind a shrub and fuck her. You don't get to watch." He sneered at Pat, but Pat saw a flicker that flashed across his face. It was there for only a moment and left Pat uncertain, confused. But, then, he fell back into the role play.

"Please don't," Pat said, panic settling in. "A-At least let me watch. I-"

"Rutabaga."

The word, the very word that Pat had heard rattling around in his head the past few weeks, came at last, bringing the whole scene to a grinding, squealing halt. But it didn't come from him. Or even Nightshade. It came from Buck—from Ezra. The deer was rubbing his dark palms along his face, hanging his head forward slightly. Nadia looked concerned, her hand going to his shoulder. Ezra chuckled, but it was with a short hitch, somewhat ragged.

"S-Sorry," he said, sliding his hands away from his face as he breathed in. "Just, uh, got a bit too real there." He paused. "I do love doing this to you, Pat. I have to put on a friendly public face all the time. Every word I say, every gesture I make is scrutinized by the media, and especially the shareholders. I can't act out. You two coming into my life has become my outlet. It… honestly feels great to be the arsehole for a change, you know?"

Pat nodded. "A-And it feels good to be the submissive," he said, quickly, wanting to cheer Ezra up. "People see me as this tall, muscle-bound dude bro. They probably take one look at Nadia and I and expect me to be the one in charge. But it couldn't be further from the truth. And while she and I know that, I doubt others would."

"Society expects certain roles from us," Ezra said nodding. "I doubt anybody would think they could take either of us in a fight," he said laughing softly. "But it sometimes…" Ezra began, pausing for a few moments, choosing his words carefully. "This roleplaying sometimes reminds me of the bullies from my past." He looked down at his hands. "I had a flash, for just a moment there, of what happened back then. Took the fun out of being the big, swinging dick. For a bit, at least."

Nadia nodded. "Should we stop? Maybe have lunch instead?"

Ezra shook his head, breathing in. "No, I just needed a short break." He smiled. "And to be reminded that *you* really do like this too, Pat."

Pat blushed, looking down. "These past few weeks, I've never been more turned on in my life," he confessed, his voice soft and hurried, as if he was worried about being stopped before he could get all the words out. "And for that, um, I thank you." He reached out and took Nadia's hand. "Even if I did need my *own* break earlier this week."

"Really?" Ezra asked, laughing softly as Pat nodded.

"It was a question of boundaries and tolerances," Nadia said, looking at Pat.

Pat turned nodded at Ezra, who looked as if his own muscles were slowly bleeding off their tension. He sagged into his chair and chuckled. "Glad I spoke up, then."

The three of them laughed—and Ezra nodded, then brushed his hands along his head. He grinned. "Ready?"

Nadia gave him a playful smile. Pat shot him a double thumbs up.

As suddenly as a gate crashing down to cover a doorway, Buck came back to the fore. He leaned forward and grinned at Pat, his eyes glittering. His hand caressed the table like a lover, touching the wood with his fingertips. His voice was husky. "So, how about you grab the bags. I think we need someone to tote our shit." He jerked his chin at the set of tote bags Pat had brought along.

Pat stood, grabbing the bags as Night rose to her feet. There was something endlessly elegant about Nightshade when she was trying her best to be alluring. She slipped her arm along Buck's, and the two walked off together with Pat trailing behind. Pat could see half the men and a quarter of the women in the food court follow Night with their eyes.

A good chunk of those women were jealous, not lustful. But there was at least one—a tomboyish mare with dyed bright pink hair—who clearly wanted to take Buck's place. Pat felt a mingling sense of pride and humiliation as he saw more than a few glances target him. He could see confusion on some faces. But then he spotted a bulky, burly-looking rhino. A familiar one. He was watching the whole affair with the wide eyes of someone who clearly did not expect to see the trio again. It was the rhino from the gym. He looked like he had parked himself at a table to get work done, a laptop swung open before him.

But after the shock faded, his eyes met Pat's. Night and Buck hadn't noticed him. Subtly, the rhino nodded to him.

Pat smiled and nodded back.

Then the trio were out of the food court and inside the shopping center.

The first place that Buck took them to was, of course, a lingerie store. The poofy poodle who stood behind the front desk was a stereotype incarnate—clapping excitedly when Nightshade mentioned she was interested in something spicy for her 'Bucky'. If the poodle was baffled by Patrick meekly standing to the side with the bags, she didn't show it.

"You would *love* this line, ma'am," she said, walking around the corner to gesture to a collection of soft-looking undergarments. Nightshade picked one up, pursing her lips, while Buck eyed the others curiously. Seeing Night's slightly disdainful sniff, the poodle scuttled over to a slightly more expensive line of deep purple, lacy things that Pat was sure had a very specific name. To him, they looked like fairly typical bras, stockings and panties. Night cooed, putting her hand against one, checking not only how it felt but the way it contrasted with her fur.

"I love it," she murmured.

"Well, lets see how you look in them," Buck said, grinning. He looked at Pat, then jerked his head at the poodle, who was looking around for more things to offer them. Pat realized Buck wanted him to distract her.

Pat gulped, then stammered. "S-So, uh, what about… those?" He pointed at a random part of the store.

"Those are socks," the poodle said plainly as Buck and Night slipped into the back room. Pat squirmed with delicious agony—the thought of Night's clothes slipping off, plopping onto the ground. Those delicious, soft breasts being cupped and squeezed. First by Buck, of course. Then, again, by her new lingerie. He noticed the poodle was looking at him, clearly waiting for a follow-up response. Pat shrugged.

"Well, of course," he said, loftily.

"You often carry bags for other people?" the poodle inquired.

Pat blushed. "Uh. Well, that's me! Super… uh… helpful guy that I am."

A few moments later, Buck emerged, a smug look on his slender muzzle. He tapped a wad of cash against the countertop, holding up a some tattered barcodes torn undergarments. The poodle looked at him with wide eyes.

"Sir!" she said, walking forward. She tried several times to start her sentence, her poofy tail slapping from side to side anxiously as she glared at him. "Did you…? You can't remove tags from store items!"

Buck smirked insolently. "They got in the way."

They hit several more stores after that. In each, Buck took delight in doing things to Nightshade that made Pat squirm. In the grocery store that was tucked into the side of the center, Buck took malicious pleasure in watching Pat's eyes as he held a rather phallic-looking strawberry to Night's lips. The sweet taste of it made her eyes close and her lips quiver. Or maybe it was the way Pat watched and squirmed that did that.

At another store, she got to try on watches. Several of them were fancier than anything Pat could have afforded. He overheard Buck's whispered comments, his arms already aching with the weight of other things that Buck had bought with careless ease.

"How long do you think it'd take dickless there to afford this?"

"All I can say is it matches the ring you gave me."

By the end of the shopping expedition, Night had gotten a new dress, new underwear, several pairs of new shoes, a new watch, and a new necklace—one that Buck had taken great pains to put around her neck, nearly grinding against her ass in public as he purred compliments in her ear. Pat was carrying all of it, the bags stuffed with other miscellaneous things that Buck had bought on a whim. As he jammed it into Buck's sleek car, Night grinned at Buck as she sprawled against the passenger seat door, her arm crooked over the roof.

"My place or yours?"

"I think the best way to end this is at yours," Buck said, grinning slightly. "That big, comfortable bed of yours…"

"Mmmm?" Night prompted, her tail almost sticking straight up in eagerness. Pat, meanwhile, was shoving his shoulder against the trunk door, trying to get it to wedge shut. While Buck's car was a sleek and fast EV, it had shit for cargo space. Once Pat had gotten the door closed, Buck started up his sentence again. He had waited until Pat could hear it.

"You need a real cock to fuck you at *least* once in a while in that bed, after all."

Pat was forced to share the back seat with the large windscreen shade that Buck used to keep the car cool while he was parked out under the sun. The seatbelt tugged at his neck and chest as he leaned his head against the felt-covered edge of the inner car. He watched as Night laughed gaily at something Buck had said. As she lounged back in her seat, Pat reached forward to squeeze her shoulder gently. She put her hand on his. He noticed the ring gleaming in the sunlight. Buck opened his mouth but Pat quickly said: "Rutabaga."

Ezra dropped the mask with an easy laugh. "Need a break?"

"Just…" Pat paused. "I love her a lot, you know?"

"I can see why," Ezra said, grinning. Then, blushing, he stammered. "T-That's not too, uh, forward, is it?"

Pat looked at Nadia.

Nadia looked back at him.

Both of them broke out laughing. Ezra joined in, his cheeks darkening further as he shook his head from side to side.

CHAPTER 12

"Really, the story ends there. We were comfortable. Happy. The journey was over.
But let's be honest. You were waiting for this part."

* * *

Ezra was the one who opened the door to the flat. Buck was the one who closed it. He grinned insolently at Nightshade, his hand cupping her muzzle, lifting her eyes to meet his. "Go back to your room and get your pretty little slutty self ready to get a real cock inside you."

"Oh *yes*," Night purred. She turned and hurried off, snatching the bags from Pat. As she walked away, Buck turned to face Pat, who was looking down at his hands, shocked that the bag handles hadn't ripped the top layer of his skin off.

"So, bitch, I got one rule for you," Buck purred. "You need to get naked."

Pat gulped. His fingers went to his collar and he undid the first few buttons. His fingers moved mechanically, without thought. His own mind was whirling, thinking of when Night had playfully pointed out how interested he was in Ezra. There was an attraction there, but he wasn't even sure what it was. His shirt slipped off and he hesitated. Buck, his bushy tail twitching with clear excitement, his thick shaft beginning to show against his khakis, smirked.

"All the way, pussy," he said. "I know you hate to compare your little pinkie prick with mine, but… well, let's be fair here. That's why Nightshade is stripping for *me*. That's why she's going to be begging for *me*. And that's why you're going to take those trousers off right *now*." His voice was a husky purr, dark like chocolate.

Pat's throat felt drier than the Sahara. His hands shook as they undid the belt. His jeans hit the floor and his six inches of hardness sprang free.

Buck shook his head with a slight smirk.

"You can touch yourself," he said casually, throwing a bone to a desperate dog. "But if you cum before I do, then you *will* be sorry. Understood?"

Pat nodded.

"I said..." Buck's voice was steady. His hand went to his ear, cupping it, as if Pat needed to be shown even the easiest instructions in the simplest ways. "Is that *understood?*"

Pat whimpered. His cock twitched and a thin line of his pre dripped to the floor, making him feel even more humiliated. Buck sneered at him and opened his mouth to continue the tirade, but Pat managed to gasp out. "Yes, I understand."

"Good," Buck said, grinning. "Come along, pussy."

The muscular deer strode through the flat as if he owned it. And considering how much money he had thrown away without thinking about it, it was entirely possible that he did. He came to the doorway that led into Pat and Night's bedroom. There, on the bed, was Nightshade in all of her glory. She was dressed in the filmy, purple lingerie. The bra cupped her breasts lovingly, pushing them upward and together, the edges of the fabric just barely above her hard nipples, accentuating their eagerness like a painter accenting a portrait's highlights. The bottoms were somewhere between a pair of panties and a thong. The dark purple did nothing to hide just how soaked and eager Night was. The stockings covered her feet and calves and parts of her knees, hooked to the undersides of the panties with thin, black straps of fabric. The stockings were sheer enough that they crept between her toes and outlined the edges of her nails. She had her hands hooked behind her neck to thrust her chest forward.

"Now that is a sight for sore eyes," Buck purred. He looked at Pat as he spread his arms. Pat blinked at him and understood what he needed to do without Buck having to say another word. Pat stepped forward, then started to undo the buttons on Buck's shirt. His fingers worked with nervous, twitching motions. He couldn't help but brush against the deer's muscular chest. Buck shifted slightly, forcing himself against Pat's body as the giraffe drew the shirt back. He practically forced Pat to inhale the musk that Night loved so much.

And that was just his shirt. Kneeling down behind him, Pat gulped and took hold of the other man's pants. He slipped the belt free, then hooked his fingers between underwear and bare fur. His member twitched hard as a rock, his head swimming slightly as Buck murmured: "Well, bitch. Get me out, get me hard."

Pat dragged Buck's pants down and his member flopped free. He was half hard; nowhere near his full length. Or girth. Pats eyes trailed from his balls to his tip and he whimpered almost as softly as Night would. Then he saw Buck looking at him past his own dick, his lips split into a wicked smirk. Pat remembered what he had said: *Get me out, get me hard.* Pat's hand shook and he slowly took hold of Buck's cock. His thick. Male. Cock. Pat's eyes closed as he focused only on the feel of him. Warm and silky smooth, and yet still hard as iron underneath, and getting harder every moment. Pat started to stroke Buck up and down, up and down, marveling at how far his hand could move before he felt the tip or the base. But then suddenly Buck slapped his hand away with a sneer.

"That's hard enough, bitch."

Buck stepped past Pat, who gazed at his hand. He had just stroked another man. The salty tang of Buck's musk hit his nostrils and he felt like he had just taken a hit of a wicked, debauched drug. He'd never have done anything like this before. Part of him was still stunned he had. But a bigger part of him—the part of him that revelled in the raw masculinity of Buck's dominant personality—delighted at the sight of Buck stepping up to the bed.

Night started to nuzzle against Buck's belly, her tongue lapping out, tracing the lines of his abdominals. Buck grinned at Pat, his hand caressing Night's long, straight hair. His fingers tugged her head back and, not breaking eye contact with Pat, he leaned forward, turning his head and catching the jackal's mouth with a deep, fierce kiss.

The stockings made it almost too easy to see Night's toes curl in delight. Her eyes rolled slightly back into her head and went soft and unfocused. When their kiss broke, tiny bits of spittle connected their lips and their tongues, catching the light shining from the lamps that lit the room in a warm, buttery glow. Gasping softly, Night whined as Buck cupped one of her breasts and squeezed. He grinned and murmured. "You want it bad, don't you bitch?"

"Yesss..." Night breathed.

"Louder," Buck purred. He leaned forward, kissing the side of her neck. His hand slipped down, fingers hooking on her panties.

"God yes," Night moaned. Then she squeaked loudly as Buck yanked. Her panties tore with a loud, rasping sound and his flat teeth caught and bit at her neck. She squirmed and thrust out one leg, her toes spreading as wide as they had once curled tightly. Her tail thumped against the bed and she grabbed onto Buck's shoulders, shuddering as the pink lips of her cunt surrounded by ebony darkness were revealed. "Ohgodohgod…" she whispered, sounding stunned by the raw, masculine power of that one movement.

Pat, meanwhile, hadn't moved. In fact, the only reason why he hadn't dropped over dead was that part of him still remembered to breathe. His heart still beat, but he felt that if he moved, if he touched himself, that he wouldn't be able to stop the torrent of cum that wanted to burst from his cock. He wouldn't even reach the bed; he'd just jizz over the floor, and the very mental image of that humiliation was enough to nearly set him off. He watched as Buck grabbed and pushed the bra down just enough to free Night's nipples. He kissed and sucked, lovingly teasing each nipple as if Night were his wife and this were their honeymoon.

Night, for her part, wasn't idle. Her hand pumped once, twice, three times up and down Buck's titanic member, slicking it with his own pre as he nibbled on a nipple, gently enough to not cause pain, but with enough force to make Night croon and gasp eagerly. Her body writhed and squirmed—but then, before she could fall to her back or spread her legs, or do much of anything else, Buck shifted his mouth. A series of lightning fast kisses mussed up and slicked her fur, leaving shining spots on her sleek darkness. Then his mouth was on her ear. He sucked on the tip as Night's eyes widened and then started to go soft. Her mouth opened and a soft, whining sound came from her. It was the sound of Night in so much pleasure that she was having a hard time processing it.

Pat gasped as he watched those strong hands, so obvious in their paleness against Night's color, cupped and squeezed her breasts. Fondled. Teased. Then Buck went to her other ear and started to kiss and nuzzle it. His tongue caught and tugged gently on the earrings that graced her sleek ears, and his hands squeezed her tightly. Her breasts molded between his strong fingers. Buck's mouth twisted into a self-satisfied smirk as Night squealed and arched her back. Her quivering thighs spread wide and her juices dripped onto the bed, slicking her thighs. It was so…

Carnal.

Raw.

It caught Pat's breath.

"Ohgod… ohgod…" Night gasped, her voice utterly breathless as Buck drew his mouth away from her ear. A single thumb pressed against her chin, lifting her head so that she looked into his eyes. As she looked up at him, Buck turned his head to look over his shoulder at Pat. He gave him the widest, cockiest, most shit-eating grin that Pat had ever seen. It made Pat's cock throb and his balls tingle. The urge to touch himself was overwhelming, but it was matched only by the power of Buck's glare. He looked at Pat with confidence, knowing that Pat would have remained perfectly still.

And Pat had.

Night's teeth nibbled at Buck's thumb tip, her crooning voice forming no words. Just desire. And so, Buck lazily looked back at her, tilted his head, and kissed her. The word kissed, though, felt so... weak. Paltry. It wasn't just a kiss, it was a conquest. It was an invasion and Night surrendered to it willingly. Her body molded to Buck's athletic chest, her back arching as his tongue slipped into her mouth, met her own, teased, played. His hands cupped her ass, squeezing her firmly as she moaned into his mouth. And it kept going. It was a kiss that wound on and on, pausing only when Night—and it was always Night—tugged away to gasp. Pant. Then get captured again. Her head turned back and Buck's muzzle fastened onto hers.

By the time Buck finally withdrew, Night's eyes were so dazzled, so dazed, that Pat was sure she hadn't a coherent thought left in her head.

"Spread your legs," Buck purred. An order. An order delivered to the most in control, dominate woman Pat had ever known. Before Pat knew it, Night had pulled her legs apart. Her whole body quivered with tiny jerks and twitches, as if she were primed and ready. And considering how sopping wet her cunt was, Pat couldn't blame her. Her hands spread her thighs slightly further apart, the lips of her sex making a slick, moist noise that made Pat's breath catch.

"Wider," Buck drawled.

Like an eager, submissive slut, Night spread her legs even further for him. Buck grinned. "Do you think you'll ever take Pat's cock again after tonight?" he spoke as he lifted up his cock and then let it drop. It slapped against her sex and her belly, the tip almost teasing her belly button. He started to grind his thick member up and down, up and down. His hips rocked with the same gentle rhythm as a boat at sea, and with the same unstoppable momentum.

"Never..." Night moaned, her back arching slightly.

Buck drew his cock back and upwards. It hung above Night, already seeming to gleam as if it had been stroked with lube. It was as slick as Pat's mouth was dry. Buck let his cock drop and slap right against her clit. Then he ground against her, teasing the folds of her sex with his member. He ground up, down, up, down; each motion accentuating just how huge he was by how wide Nightshade's pussy became just accepting the tip of his shaft. He drew it back slightly, looking amused at the way Night eagerly panted and moaned.

"You've gotten so used to taking me, I bet you can't even feel him anymore," he purred.

"I-I know…" Night turned her head to the side. She looked ashamed. And eager.

"Mmm…" Buck chuckled. Then he bumped his cock against her sex. Night hissed softly in response. "Damn, I forgot how *tight* you are, love. You let the pencil dick fuck you a few times, and you get tight again, don't you?" Buck shook his head. "Fuck this." He looked at Pat. "Dickless, get your hands off your *clit* and come over here."

Pat, who had finally worked up the courage to grip his own dick at least a little, jerked forward, his hands releasing his own aching, throbbing member as if it had turned red hot. Standing near Buck reminded Pat of the crackling charge that seemed to surround the muscular deer. His musk and the sweet scent of Nightshade's arousal mixed together in Pat's nostrils, making his head swim. He didn't know if he could say no to anything right now. Buck grinned at him, and part of Pat wondered if he should be afraid.

And then Buck removed all doubt.

"Dock me," he said.

"W-What?" Pat asked.

"I don't feel like forcing my way in and grinding around…" Buck shook his head. "I figure, you're here. You can do the scut work. Fuck, you already got me hard enough. Dock my cock in your girl." As he spoke, he put his hands on the bed, taking his weight onto his knees as he crawled over Nightshade. He leaned forward, kissing Night as deeply as he had before, while she moaned in clear ecstasy. Her back arched and her thighs spread so wide that Pat was shocked that he didn't hear bones popping. Pat gulped and stepped forward. Hesitantly, he reached towards the cock that had been the center of his sex life for almost a month.

His hands closed around Buck's cock. He had held his member a mere few minutes ago, but that had felt like an eternity of exquisite agony, and so he felt a kind of shock as he took it up once again. He knew what it felt like, but it still awed him. Silkiness wrapped around a length of hardness that made him think about touching molten iron. The tip of Buck's cock dribbled a line of pre-cum thicker than Pat's own ejaculations, soaking the sheets between Night's thighs. Pat moaned softly as he lifted Buck's cock upwards, slipping him against Nightshade.

"Hold me steady, bitch," Buck said, his voice a soft purr. As he spoke, his hips started to drive forward. Pat held him steady, his palms shaking as he felt the thickness of Buck's member sinking deeper and deeper into his lover. Night moaned and whimpered with each inch, her sex spreading wider and wider; Buck taking a few moments every two or so inches to shift and squirm, widening her further, until at last, every inch of that footlong prick was buried in her cunt.

Pat now had a pair of large, virile balls in his hands. He kept them there, too terrified of fucking up the scene to worry about his own heterosexuality.

"Mmm, that's just the perfect place for those hands of yours," Buck murmured. "Feel 'em?" He chuckled as Pat whimpered. The massive deer shifted himself slightly, settling himself deep inside Night, who looked as if she was having the next best thing to a religious experience. Pat's breath caught as he felt the slight shifting of Buck's balls in his palms. He couldn't help himself. He squeezed gently and Buck crooned, drawing his cock back. This pressed the underside of his cock against Pat's knuckles, slicking them with Night's juices.

"Like getting your hands on a real pair?" Buck hissed.

He slammed back home and his balls were drawn slightly taut against Pat's hands. Pat felt a jolt of fear, but Buck rolled his head back and groaned in what sounded like abject pleasure. Pat continued to squeeze and fondle the balls, his tongue darting out. He wasn't sure if he was going to lick his own lips or…

"Oh Buck! Oh *Buck!*" Night moaned loudly, her ears flattening back against her head. "Please, fuck me harder. I wanna have *bruises*, Buck!" She drove her hips back against the cock as if she needed it more than fucking oxygen.

Buck laughed, then started to redouble his efforts. His cock slammed into her again and again, his balls surging and twitching in Pat's palm. He started to get into a rhythm, squeezing him at just the right moment to wring a quiet grunt of happiness from the deer. He felt so utterly subservient, so utterly cucked, that it almost blew his mind. Pat felt depraved and degraded and joyful all at once. The joy shocked him, but he felt it growing brighter and brighter in his belly as he watched Night writhe and gasp, yelp and moan, groan and whimper. Night's powerful orgasms would squeeze Buck out of her, making Pat quickly reinsert the massive cock back inside, only to watch it pop out from another wave of pleasure hitting her. She was enraptured.

Then it clicked.

He felt joy because Nightshade was feeling joy. It was the utter happiness of complete abandonment of jealousy by embracing jealousy. He had earlier thought Night was having a religious experience, but what he felt now was hard to put into any other context. His breath caught and he squeezed Buck's balls at just the right moment. He felt it in that moment; felt it in his bones, in his soul.

The virile cervine pumped into Nightshade quickly before hilting himself one last time, throwing his head back and roaring in pleasure. His antlers glinted in the light of the lamps, but Pat only had eyes for those firm balls in his palms. He could feel them clench and growing taut, tight as a drum. Pat would have called it a flood of cum, but that might have undersold it. Semen burst from around the tightness of Nightshade's pussy lips, shockingly white against her dark smoothness. It slicked against her thighs, soaking into her fur, puddling along the curve of her ass, and making her tail sticky and tacky. It dripped and flowed and surged, soaking into Pat's hands as he clutched onto Buck's balls just tightly enough to feel every surging pulse.

Because Buck didn't just spurt once. He kept spurting and spurting, and each and every throb seemed to force more of the cum out of Night's desperately full cunt. Soon, Pat's hands felt like they had been painted from fingertips to wrists in Buck's cum.

He pulled his hands back, wonderingly, looking at them. He felt the boiling heat of Buck's semen dripping along the inside of his wrists, following the curve of his spots.

Softly, Buck panted. Breaking the silence of the moment, his voice rasped out the mocking question: "Gonna taste it?"

Pat's tongue lolled out of his mouth. His head seemed to spin and he wasn't sure what he was thinking; it came in incoherent spurts and wriggles as he heard Nightshade croon.

"Noooo, I wannnt itttt…" Nightshade moaned, her voice desperately needy. Pat stood shakily, his rock hard cock bobbing as he walked over. Night took hold of one of his wrists and dragged his hand to her mouth. She started to lap and lick and suck at his fingers. Her nose bumped against his palm and she got a bit of white on it, as if she were drinking too greedily from a cup of milk. She quickly switched to the other hand. Her tongue flicked again and again as her muzzle pressed to Pat's fingers so desperately that her teeth almost rasped against his flesh. Then, slowly, she drew her mouth back, panting quietly.

Buck drew out of her. Cum oozed from her sex. Night slowly sprawled herself back. She panted heavily as she looked at the ceiling. Her eyes were unfocused and she twitched with the aftershocks of a string of her own orgasms. Buck looked down at her with a slow smile. Then he looked back at Pat, who remained on the very edge—his cock twitching, his body quivering. Cum wanted to escape, but he was gripping the very base of his dick and holding his breath. Buck sneered at him.

"Ready for round two?"

"Round what?" Pat squeaked.

"Oh yessss…" Night breathed.

Buck jerked his head. "On your hands and knees, love. I wanna fuck you doggy style. Seems appropriate for a bitch like you, huh?" He chuckled, and Night nodded, almost desperately eager. Pat's eyes widened as he saw that Buck's cock was still half hard, and he was stroking himself back to full hardness, as if his body had no need for a refractory period. But before Pat could draw back, Buck's eyes transfixed him. His grin was malicious.

"And you. Under her."

Pat laid back without a word of protest nor a moment's hesitation. Night swung a leg over him. As she moved, cum oozed and dripped from her well-fucked pussy. It flecked across Pat's belly and dribbled over his cock, hot as candle wax. Pat's eyes fluttered and he shuddered as his lover's warm breasts grazed his chest. She was swaying over him. The glint of Buck's ring shown out of the corner of Pat's eye as Night pressed her hands on either side of his head. But before she could speak, Buck was looming over both of them. His hand cupped her head, turning it to the side. His mouth pressed to hers for another one of those soul-devouring kisses.

Something Pat hadn't quite realized before was how… messy they were. Spittle dripped onto his face, sizzling hot and dragging whimpers from him as his tongue darted out, slicking along his lips. Then Buck shoved Night's head away from his, growling as he did so. His fingers worked through her hair and he pushed her down to make her kiss Pat. He had never felt this before; it was as if it weren't Night kissing him. She only did it because her face was pressed to his. Because of...

Him.

Her tongue thrust into his mouth and Pat cupped her breasts, squeezing her, but only for a few seconds. That was because Buck, leaning back on his haunches, had his hands free to push his palms underneath Pat's. Even those breasts belonged to him. The backs of Pat's hands rested against Buck's palms and he felt the cervine's strength squeezing Nightshade. It was Buck that moaned through her mouth, it was Buck that made her kiss more wildly and frantically. It was Buck that let Nightshade pull back and allow Pat to gasp and pant for air.

Night's sex was right above Pat's cock—which was hard enough to pound down nails. But it was Buck's dick that was once again sliding into her, inch by glorious inch, pushing more oozing cum out of her drenched orifice, making it paint Pat's groin in hot stickiness.

And then Buck twisted the knife. "Mmm... room for one more," he breathed.

Pat's eyes bulged.

"She's a desperate bitch, our lovely Nightshade," Buck purred. His antlers glinted as he lifted his head back. "She's gotten so used to me, she needs more cock to fill her up. You're insatiable, aren't you my dear?"

Night didn't say yes so much as she threw her head back and screamed it. Not in words, but in the sound of another shattering orgasm. Her breasts molded to Pat's chest, her nipples grinding against his as she panted, hot and desperate, in his face. Pat grabbed his own dick and pushed upwards as Buck thrust onwards. Guided by instinct and his own palm, Pat slipped into Nightshade. His eyes widened as he felt the tight folds of her sex pushing him against the thick, silk-steel shaft of Buck. The closeness was so intense that their hearts beat as one, the throbbing of their sexes in perfect sync.

Night sucked in her breath, her eyes opening wide as she stared ahead in disbelief at the sensation of having both men inside her. Then, slowly, her eyes closed and her breathing came back in a soft whimper as she relaxed and shifted her hips to angle the dual cocks into optimum position.

Buck and Pat began to alternate, sawing in and out of Night. She moaned and writhed, her eyes closed, her ears firmly laid back against her skull as she drooled onto Pat's face, her eyes utterly mindless when they did manage to flutter open in thin slits. Her whole body quivered, and Pat had no words for the feelings surging through him. Buck's enormous, silkened rod fucked Pat as much as Night, brushing against him, sending electricity through his body. The cock-to-cock contact, enfolded by the woman he loved, was too intense. But Buck was the one who had been thrusting first. And he wasn't holding back.

He came.

This time, the amount of cum was merely impressive, rather than legendary. But the feeling was infinitely more personal now. It rushed around Pat's member, surging and enveloping his cock before spilling out of Night's pussy and dripping along his balls. He shuddered and writhed against this unfamiliar lubricant. Buck laughed and gasped as he drew himself out of Night. She, in turn, started to sit herself down on Pat's cock. Her eyes met his.

"Ruta… baga…" She breathed.

Ezra sagged. In relief? Merely because he was tired? Pat had no idea.

Nadia only had eyes for Pat in this moment. And he had eyes only for her. Her eyes were unfocused and eager. The same kind of cock drunk look she had when nuzzling against Buck's member in the office. She leaned her head forward and breathed her words on Pat's face. "I… I need… *you.*"

Not your cum. Not your dick.

You.

Pat thrust into her with strength he didn't know he had. It wasn't the strength of muscles, it was the movement of passion, and he had never in his life needed Nadia more than this. The safeword had stripped away all pretense, all titles. The rest of the room fell away as his brown eyes met her beautiful, endlessly green ones. He was drowning in her and he never wanted to breathe again. They couldn't kiss, they couldn't even speak. To do anything less than this… this perfect, beautiful moment, would feel like sacrilege.

Nadia quivered around him and Pat let himself go. This wasn't a moment that could be drawn out. To do anything but live it…

No.

Pat closed his eyes to slits. Tears brimmed in them. Hot, salty droplets in turn slipped along Nadia's muzzle. She sobbed, the emotion too powerful for anything else. Then their bodies met one last time. Her breasts mashed to his chest, and her hands slipped under him to cling to his back. Her nails dug in and Pat welcomed the pain, for it was just more closeness.

He shuddered and came. His balls clenched and his own arms crushed Nadia against him. He knew that it was too tight, but anything less than the whole of his being wasn't enough.

Then, slowly, the feeling of completeness receded.

And Pat became aware…

That he was bleeding on the sheets.

"Oh my God!" Nadia barked as Pat shifted a bit and revealed the blood.

Ezra started, then exclaimed: "I'll get some disinfectant!" He turned and bounded out of the room, but Nadia was already pushing at Pat's back. Pat sat forward, hissing softly while trying to say that he was fine at the same time. Nadia's eyes brimmed with tears as she nuzzled against his shoulders.

"I'm so sorry," she whispered.

"Heyyy," Pat crooned. "Vicky had warned me this was a risk when dating a carnivore. But it's worth it." He winced as Nadia's nose bumped against one of his cuts. Then he hissed, but not in pain, as her tongue darted out. She licked his wounds in gentle, slow, cleansing laps. Pat shivered and remembered how when they first started dating, she had left similar wounds. He chuckled softly and whispered: "You left way smaller ones this time. Much better about your claws."

Nadia snorted, but it was a wet snort.

"I love you, Pat," she said. Her voice sounded thick and choked.

Pat reached back. He found her hand without needing to look, without needing to grope. He just held it. He squeezed.

"I love you, Nadia."

Then Ezra bustled in, holding disinfectant, cotton balls, and bandages. Nadia drew back, and Ezra quickly daubed disinfectant onto the wounds as Pat stammered out that he didn't need it. But it was too late. The disinfectant rushed in and burned, and Pat squirmed and hissed, while trying to not look like a total baby. Five bandages later and Pat was wincing as he leaned back against the pillow. "I don't know if we needed to go this far. They were really tiny cuts!" He grinned as Ezra shook his head in response, looking quite stern about it all.

"Do you know how my reputation would look if I let the man writing an article about me get ill from an infection?" he said, his voice so serious that Pat wondered if he was joking. The moment of panicked realization had actually been something of a blessing. The intense sensations that had

filled Patrick and Nadia in that moment had been unsustainable. But Pat hadn't known how to navigate his way out of that headspace. Being punctured a bit helped, and now it felt as if a new mood had settled over him. It was somewhere between the high after a good run, the delight after a long bath, and the joy after good sex. A melange of happiness.

Nadia crawled onto the bed next to him. Her voice was slightly raw from the number of times she had screamed her pleasure out. She nuzzled her nose against Pat's bicep, then pushed his arm up with her muzzle to get her nose against his armpit. Her ears flicked back and she whispered a quiet string of words that might have been apologies. Pat slipped his arm around her shoulders, tugging her in close.

Ezra sat down next to her on the bed, looking unsure.

He was still naked, and at this moment, Pat wasn't sure how he felt about the other man's body. He knew that he was well past discomfort, so he grinned and motioned with his head.

"Come on, Ezra. Get over here."

Ezra's big deer ears perked up, and then he crawled forward. Soon, a very happy Nadia was sandwiched between two excellent examples of the masculine form. She looked as happy as a bug in a rug, her eyes closed, tail lazily wagging, her whole body buzzing with contentment. Pat was happy too. His right hand caressed her belly, while his left was crooked up to caress one of her ear tips. Ezra nuzzled her other ear, and his palm worked alongside her scalp, fingers tugging against her hair.

"Iiiiiii could get uuuuuuused to this," Nadia cooed.

"Well, I'm sorry, Night," Ezra said.

"Nadia," she murmured, lazily.

"N-Nadia?" Ezra asked.

"Well, I wasn't born Nightshade, my parents weren't *mental*," Nadia mumbled with a smirk, her muzzle almost touching her chest as she let her head loll forward. Her eyes were closed.

"Are you heading somewhere?" Pat asked Ezra, feeling his heart skip a beat.

Ezra smiled, slightly. "Hopefully. We're in the crunch time to get the latest heavy launcher up. I plan to be upon the second one." He chuckled. "I'd be on the first, but my shareholders weren't happy about that."

"You're going to be on a rocket?" Pat asked, his brow furrowing.

"Well, it'll have a small shuttle attached. These days, CEOs have to build the brand with our own faces, you know?"

Nadia snickered. "I dunno. Seems kinda gauche to me."

Ezra looked faintly offended, then each of them laughed, but there was a tinge of sadness at the same time. They cuddled and kissed, but never quite worked up the energy to go for a round three. They felt drained and happy. Ezra chatted with Nadia about her day job. Pat showed Ezra some of his nerdiest books. Nadia demonstrated her newest dance moves once her knees started working again. And they spent what felt like hours petting her. Pat worried, sometimes, that she might get bored of just laying there while the two men groomed her fur. She never did.

In the end, dawn came and Ezra had to get dressed to leave.

"Goodbye, Ezra," Nadia said, sitting up. She moved to stand, but Ezra held up his hand, stopping her. He grinned at them.

"Don't get up for me. The two of you... You're too goddamn beautiful like that." He paused. Then he kicked at the ground and clasped his hands behind his back. "Thank you."

"Thank us? Thank *you!*" Pat laughed.

"No, I mean..." Ezra shook his head. "I've never felt this kind of connection before. It was intense and special and... just..." He sighed. "Thank you. Thank you for letting me get a glimpse into your relationship. Thank you for letting me see what you have. Even if it was only for this moment." He smiled. "It almost makes me want to stay..."

"Almost?" Nadia asked, her voice soft.

Ezra paused, then breathed out a slow sigh. He nodded. "Almost."

Nadia looked at Pat. Pat looked at her. He nodded slightly.

Nadia leaned forward and kissed Pat. It was a short, fierce kiss. Then she stood and, with her tongue still tasting like Pat, kissed Ezra. The deer stood stock still, his eyes wide as saucers. He looked nothing like Buck in that moment. Instead, all Pat could see was the nerdy cervine who had been teased for his antlers, shocked that anyone would want him. Nadia drew her mouth back and whispered something in his ear. Pat never asked what she had said. There was a place for privacy, even in this moment. Ezra looked punch drunk. He smiled, whispered back to Nadia. Then he turned.

And left.

And they never saw him again. In person, at least.

He was on TV often enough, though. Usually in a spacesuit, waving at the camera.

EPILOGUE

"And thus… we bucked the system."

* * *

"Too corny of an ending?"

Nadia spun the chair away from the desk, tapping her pen against her muzzle. "Definitely corny. And the title? *Bucking the System?* Pretty on the nose." She grinned. "But no, I don't think you gave away *too* much of our personal lives. I also love that you made me a vixen."

"Well, I couldn't use our real identities. Imagine if I wrote Ezra's role as a deer. A famous, billionaire, deer businessman? There's only so many of those. That's why I made him a stallion, changed his profession and made him only modestly rich. And since I had changed him, I figured why not have fun changing all of us around?"

"Hence why you're a goat?" Nadia asked, smirking. Then, she said seriously: "But no. I think… I think that kink magazine will love this. What was it called again?"

"The Masque," Pat said, as he stood, picking up the manuscript. He had printed it so that Nadia could make notes and corrections. In addition to corrections and suggestions, she had doodled hearts around the bits she liked the most. Pat's eyes fell on the opening lines of first page, after the disclaimer that the names and species had been changed to protect privacy.

My day was bracketed by the two of them. The events went into motion when I saw her off and later met him.

Drawn underneath were a trio of hearts and a great big smiley face.

With that, Pat winked at Nadia and gave her a kiss, then left to make the corrections on his computer. A gleam caught his eye and he looked at a glass container on the dresser that held the gold ring Ezra had gifted Night. A keepsake to remember him by, in addition to all the memories.

He enjoyed the day. A bright, sunny day. A day that seemed ready to go on forever. A day for lovers.

A day for Night.

THE END

Bucking the System

Nightshade & Patrick

Bucking the System

Otter & Rhino

About the Authors

Dragon Cobolt

A mysterious and powerful dragon dwelling in a large, possibly misty mountain, Dragon Cobolt has a massive pile of gold and a yen for writing. Writing and putting his/her (being a shapeshifter has its advantages) stories out in the marketplace since late 2016, Dragon Cobolt is just glad to entertain.

He sometimes masquerades as a humble human, and uses the facade that Dragon Cobolt is merely an internet persona to throw adventuring parties off his tail.

Kadath

Coffee, zombies, giraffes. These sum up the interests of Kadath, an artist specializing in erotic anthropomorphic comics. He's been illustrating stories set in his *Londoners* universe for over a decade. His online presence is that of a be-speckled giraffe, toiling away at smut for the masses.

Kadath currently lives in the rainy, coffee-abundant Seattle area, with his longtime girlfriend and artistic collaborator Kaylii, along with their cat, Niko.

About the Book

In 2017, Kadath made a comic called *Dirty Talk* which featured two of his most popular characters, Patrick and Nightshade, engaging in a fantasy cuckolding scenario. Inspired by this, Dragon Cobolt expressed interest in writing a follow-up where the fantasy became reality. The publisher Kadath worked with announced a cuckolding-themed anthology, and Kadath was preparing to ask Dragon Cobolt to write that follow-up story as a submission to the book. Unfortunately, the anthology was cancelled, but Kadath approached Dragon Cobolt with the proposal anyway, it was accepted, and the short story blossomed into a novella. While the characters and setting are based on Kadath's *Londoners* comics, the story and newly-introduced characters are Dragon Cobolt's own creations. Kadath provided character and cover art for the finished project, bringing Dragon Cobolt's ideas to life.